He quirked a dark eyebrow at her. "You don't allow men to open doors for you?"

"I can open my own doors." She was being pigheaded, and she knew it. She let men open doors for her all the time if they offered.

She saw a glint of something dangerous in his eyes. Something exciting. "Yes, I'm sure that you can. But as of today you are my woman. And that means that I will treat you as I would treat a lover, *bella mia.*"

He purred the endearment, and she felt it vibrate all the way down to her toes. Her knees wobbled slightly and she gave in, sinking into the car's plush leather seats to avoid giving herself away.

An arrogant grin lit his handsome features. "Now, let's go find you a ring. Something to show the world that you are mine."

All about the author...
Maisey Yates

MAISEY YATES knew she wanted to be a writer, even before she knew what it was she wanted to write.

At her very first job she was fortunate enough to meet her very own tall, dark and handsome hero, who happened to be her boss, and promptly married him and started a family. It wasn't until she was pregnant with her second child that she found her very first Harlequin Presents® in a local thrift store—by the time she'd reached the happily ever after, she had fallen in love. She devoured as many as she could get her hands on after that, and she knew that these were the books she wanted to write!

She started submitting and nearly two years later, while pregnant with her third child, she received The Call from her editor. At the age of twenty-three she sold her first manuscript to Harlequin Presents, and she was very glad that the good news didn't send her into labor!

She still can't quite believe she's blessed enough to see her name on not just any book, but on her favorite books.

Maisey lives with her supportive, handsome, wonderful, diaper-changing husband and three small children across the street from her parents and the home she grew up in, in the wilds of southern Oregon. She enjoys the contrast of living in a place where you might wake up to find a bear on your back porch, then walk into the home office to write stories that take place in exotic, urban locales.

His Virgin Acquisition **is Maisey Yates's
first novel for Harlequin Presents!**

Maisey Yates

HIS VIRGIN ACQUISITION

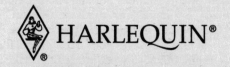

HARLEQUIN®

TORONTO • NEW YORK • LONDON
AMSTERDAM • PARIS • SYDNEY • HAMBURG
STOCKHOLM • ATHENS • TOKYO • MILAN • MADRID
PRAGUE • WARSAW • BUDAPEST • AUCKLAND

Recycling programs
for this product may
not exist in your area.

ISBN-13: 978-0-373-12949-2

HIS VIRGIN ACQUISITION

First North American Publication 2010.

HIS VIRGIN ACQUISITION

To the MH mavens, my dear sisters.

Thanks for your insight, your support, and most of all your friendship.

And to my husband, Haven. Without you I wouldn't know what romance is.

CHAPTER ONE

"I THINK the numbers speak for themselves. Marriage is definitely the most profitable course of action."

It seemed Elaine Chapman had finally come to the end of her lengthy presentation.

Marco De Luca scanned the expanse of his office, looking for hidden cameras or some other sign that she was here on assignment from a reality show. There was no way she could be serious.

He didn't spot a blinking camera light anywhere, nor did he detect an ounce of insincerity in her tone. He stopped his search and locked his eyes onto her determined face. She *was* serious. Although why that should come as a shock he wasn't sure. Ms. Chapman was known for using whatever means necessary to get ahead. Including her body.

Marco's gaze swept her up and down. "Marriage? To you?"

Elaine's face heated at the incredulous note in his voice. She knew she wasn't exactly Miss New York. Clearly Marco did too, as she seemed to recall reading somewhere that he'd once *dated* Miss New York, but she wasn't *that* bad.

"Of what benefit could that possibly be to me?"

He leaned back in his chair and put his hands behind his head, delineating muscles that weren't at all concealed by his tame button-up dress shirt. She forced her eyes back to his face. Who cared about his muscles? So he had them? Men did, after all. She did not need this distraction right now, or ever.

"Didn't you pay attention to the chart?" She held up the colored graph for his further inspection.

"I heard what you said. But none of it was worth hearing. I've allowed you to waste twenty minutes of my valuable time, time that you couldn't begin to afford to re-imburse me for, and the business proposal you were sup-posed to come here and offer me turns out to be a marriage proposal? You're lucky I haven't called Security."

He studied the tired, bleak-looking woman standing in front of him. He had only seen her on a few occasions, and even then it had been from a distance, but every time, even at formal charity balls, she had been in some variation of a black or navy blue pantsuit, her blond hair scraped back into a tight, unforgiving bun.

She was one of those women. The kind who seemed to think that they had to look like a man in order to compete in the business world. The sort of woman who took great care to disguise every trace of femininity she possessed. And this one did a particularly excellent job. He also knew that if she *could* use her femininity to her advantage she would do so without shame or scruples. Though he hadn't experienced that personally.

"I've already explained how it benefits you." She straightened her shapeless suit jacket and continued. "You're a smart man, Mr. De Luca. You want the bottom line, so here it is: married men make more money than single men. That's a fact. And you can't pretend the statistic doesn't interest you. Your reputation for expanding your company at almost any cost is legendary. A marriage between the two of us is a business strategy. A valid one."

James Preston. The name swam through his mind. James was holding out on a multi-million-dollar deal because he couldn't imagine handing over his beloved resort to a man who had no concept of the joys of a loving family. So instead he was out to find some family man to take it over. A family man who would have neither the time nor the drive that Marco had to offer the resort. Marco wanted the deal, no denying that, and as it stood he wasn't going to get it. It had been gnawing at him for weeks. He didn't do failure. Not anymore. He'd had enough of it.

But marriage seemed like an extreme solution; he'd spent thirty-three years avoiding the institution, and he had no desire to enter into it now.

"And you honestly think I'm going to stoop to marrying you to increase my profit margins?"

She pursed her lips, clearly unhappy with his choice of words. "Yes. I do. You're a legend in the industry. Not just for all that you've achieved, although that's impressive enough, but also for your ruthlessness, and that is something we share. Although my aim is considerably lower."

"And how does this benefit you, Ms. Chapman?" He stood up from his position behind the desk and walked around to the other side of it, so he was standing directly in front of her, his arms crossed. "Because, businesswoman that you are, there has to be an angle."

Elaine took a deep breath to steady herself. She had answers to all of his objections carefully prepared, but being on the receiving end of his intense dark gaze caused her well-rehearsed argument to get jumbled in her head.

She had never seen a man as gorgeous as he was on

this side of the silver screen. He was the epitome of tall, dark and handsome, and he made her want to ditch her normally feminist persona in favor of that of a swooning Southern belle.

Swooning? Where had that come from? She'd never swooned in her life! She wasn't even sure what swooning was.

She tried to collect her thoughts and continue on as rehearsed, but it was hard to concentrate when he was standing so close being all tall and handsome and intimidating and *handsome*. His masculinity was so potent it nearly reached out and grabbed her, or made her want to reach out and grab him. She had never had a fantasy before that she could recall, and here she was in the middle of a business presentation, entertaining predatory thoughts about the man to whom she was making her pitch. He was throwing her completely off balance.

She was starting to think she'd made a serious miscalculation. A very serious, very tall, very sexy miscalculation.

Taking a deep breath to banish her rogue thoughts, she pressed on, "My father, like most men his age, thinks a woman's place is in the kitchen. And while I have no problem with a woman being in the kitchen, if that's what she wants, it's not what I want. *I* want the company, and he doesn't seem to think I'm capable of running it."

"*Are* you capable of running a company?" He leaned back against the desk and her eyes were drawn to his big hands, which were clutching the edge of the desk, supporting his weight. They were nice hands, masculine and callused. She hated smooth hands on a man. Well, theoretically she hated smooth hands on a man. Actually, she hadn't given it much thought before.

She was letting herself get distracted again. This was not the time for latent hormones to be popping up and making themselves known. She wanted this. She needed this. Attractive or not, she was not letting this man stand in her way.

She drew up to her full height, which in her chunky heels put her at the bottom of his chin. "I am more than capable, and more than qualified. I have a business degree, I interned at a Fortune 500 company, and I'm currently working as the head accountant for a small marketing firm. You can rest assured that, with or without those qualifications, if I were my father's son he would hand over the reins of the company to me with pride."

"If you're so incredibly competent why haven't you simply branched out on your own?"

Her lips, lush when they weren't pinned together in an uncompromising line, tightened, and she narrowed her eyes. "I would have. But my father had me sign a non-compete clause when I worked for him back when I was in college. I'm banned from starting a new business that might compete in any way with Chapman Electronics."

"And you were foolish enough to sign it?"

He enjoyed watching the pink flush creep into her ivory cheeks. It made him wonder if she flushed the same color when she was aroused, which made him wonder just what it would take to arouse passion in a woman like Elaine. Spreadsheets, most likely.

"At the time I assumed the business would pass to me when he retired, so it seemed like a non-issue," she said curtly.

"And you think that a marriage of convenience is going to help you out of this little situation you've landed yourself in?"

"I told you, I've done my research." She took a step

closer to him and put her hands on her hips, pulling that awful jacket tight, revealing a small waist and the gentle rounding of her breasts. "You're set to acquire my father's company upon his retirement."

"And how exactly does marriage work to your advantage?"

"The contracts have already been signed, haven't they?" He nodded in confirmation. "So he can't back out now."

"Well, he could try, but it would be unpleasant for him." His voice held a hard edge that left her in little doubt that he was telling the truth. He seemed completely ruthless. She liked that.

"So I marry you, and as your wife I'll own half of your assets, which makes me half-owner of my father's business. I would have come to simply negotiate a sale, but there's a clause in your contract that says if you sell to me you'll forfeit the company."

"Yes, I am aware of the clause you're talking about. I got a little bit of a chuckle out of it, actually. But I had to wonder if it was added because of your gender or your competence." His deep, mildly accented voice held a hint of mockery that made her bristle.

"My father is the consummate male chauvinist. Ideally I'd send him to a therapist to explore his issues, and maybe we could reach some sort of agreement that way," she said dryly. "But that isn't likely. So here I am. My father's a good businessman, a worthy adversary. But I'm better. I found a loophole, a rather gaping one. The contract says I can't *buy* the business, however, there isn't anything in there about me inheriting the company—say, through a divorce." She couldn't disguise the self-satisfied note that had crept into her voice.

She studied his face, searching for a hint as to what he

might be thinking, but there was nothing. The man was solid granite.

Marco laconically flipped through her stack of data. "It seems to me, Ms. Chapman, that you've presented a one-sided deal. You get your family company and I get what? An increase in profits based on hypothetical statistics? I don't think so. That's not how business is done."

He took great satisfaction in seeing her unflappable cool slip for a moment. "I know how business is done," she snapped. "I'm fully qualified. I went to Harvard."

"Time in a classroom does not teach you the reality of the business world. You know numbers. You know text-book scenarios. You don't know how things really work. As proved by your willingness to sign whatever piece of paper your father put in front of you."

She thrust her chin up in a gesture of defiance. "I know how things work. Money makes the world turn. And this will mean money for you. You'll make more in gross profit from this than you ever could have made with my father's small potatoes business. Chapman Electronics barely makes fifteen percent of what *one* of the De Luca Corporation's subsidiaries pulls in annually. Marrying me has the poten-tial to boost profits by ten percent in each of the companies owned and operated by the De Luca empire."

The tip of her tongue darted out and slicked over her bottom lip. Her lips were actually very full and tempting when they weren't pinched together. He could easily imagine them parting beneath his own as she granted him entry into her mouth. Imagine her shedding some of her hardened shell and melting beneath him.

She did a wonderful job of downplaying her natural femininity. Such a good job that most people would miss it entirely. But natural beauty like hers was impossible to bury completely. She had large, generously lashed china-blue eyes, finely arched eyebrows, and clear pale skin. She wasn't made-up and finished to a highly glossed sheen like the women he typically went out with, but there was a freshness to her look that intrigued him.

It had been a long time since a woman had intrigued him at all. In his experience women were all very much the same in the presence of a rich man. Flirtatious, transparent and, once the sparkle wore off, boring.

"And how long do you see such a marriage lasting?" It was the sheer mercenary quality of the proposition that had him asking questions. It was interesting to meet someone as committed, as driven as he was, to the pursuit of success.

"Certainly not 'till death do us part'. I figure twelve months should be enough to make it look as though we gave it a legitimate try. Sadly…" she gave a little shrug of one of her padded shoulders "…as happens with more than fifty percent of marriages, ours just didn't stand the test of time."

This was where the real bottom line was revealed. He still didn't believe she would want only Chapman Electronics. She was right in her assessment of it as small potatoes. And a woman who was willing to sell her body for a contract would not be interested in small potatoes.

"And after that twelve months is when you think you'll get your hefty settlement? Are you going to cry abuse? Say that I was unfaithful?"

"Hardly! I told you I want the company. Nothing more or less than that."

"But what will become of my newly increased profits when we divorce?"

"That's the beauty of it," she said, her smile had become a smirk. "When your wife leaves you and breaks your poor heart, your profits will increase even more. I've done my research."

"So you've said."

She gave him a pained look and continued. "Empathy is a very powerful emotion. Most of the men you'll be doing business with have been divorced, generally because commitment to their business outweighed commitment to their wife. When your wife leaves you, you'll have the whole lot of them standing around ready to dole out cigars and sympathy."

Everything in him was on high alert. His blood was pumping faster, just as it did when he knew he was on to a profitable deal. He lived for this. Lived for the challenge—the danger, even. And it wasn't in him to shy away from either.

He didn't need more money. No question. But he wanted it. The boy who had slept in grimy alleyways and crowded homeless shelters craved the security. Needed to push farther and farther away from those low points, keep pushing past all that he had been. Needed constant success, where before there had only been failure and struggle.

"There would have to be a prenup. And don't think for one moment I'll be content to let you or your lawyer draw it up and start making demands. The way I see it, I could send you out the door and I will have lost nothing. You, on the other hand, will have lost everything. Where I only stand to gain, you could lose."

She was slightly shocked that he seemed to be on the verge of accepting her offer. Obviously she had hoped that he would, but a very large part of her hadn't believed she had a prayer. "I have no issue with you having a prenup drafted. I don't want anything from you but what's rightfully mine."

He looked her up and down in a way that made her feel as if she was on the auction block.

"Would we be consummating this marriage?" It seemed important to know. Surprisingly, he found his body responding to the idea. The faint hint of a figure he'd caught lurking under her masculine attire was more than a little enticing. And there was something about her high-necked don't-touch-me blouse that just begged to have the buttons released one by one…

He was amused when a tide of color crept up her neck and rushed into her cheeks. He hadn't seen a woman blush since… Well, maybe never. The women he associated with were not the blushing kind. They were like him—jaded when it came to life and relationships. He liked a woman who knew how to please a man. A woman who understood that sex was not love. A woman who knew the score.

Normally he didn't go for the whole bashful innocent façade, and he knew it *was* a façade, but somehow she was even more beautiful when she blushed. The layers of composed, hard-edged businesswoman seemed to fall away and reveal a woman who was capable of being soft and sexy.

"No!" She hadn't meant to sound so flustered by his question, but she wasn't a good enough actress to pretend she was unaffected by his blatant mention of sex. The topic wasn't exactly something she was used to discussing in the broad light of day with a man. Or with anyone, at any time. "I mean you're free to do whatever you want, with *whoever* you want. With discretion, of course. I sincerely doubt that any of those conservative old businessmen would have any sympathy for you if they knew you had been running around…philandering behind your wife's back!"

He let his eyes wander over her body, and he suddenly

saw the appeal of women concealing more than they revealed. It was making him unbearably curious.

He wondered what it would take to get her to loosen up a little, to get her to let her hair down. He could picture her with her blond hair loose around her face; her cheeks flushed pink with passion, her gorgeous mouth swollen from kisses. His kisses. She would be an aggressive lover, he decided. A woman so bound and determined to give as good as she got in the boardroom would very likely behave the same in the bedroom.

He felt himself getting hard thinking about it. He let his eyes wander over her figure, catching hints of the lushness that lay beneath her loose cut clothing. Oh, yes, beneath that armor she was all woman. Slender, yet soft and curvy.

"Whoever I want?" He lowered his voice and brushed his knuckles gently across her cheek.

Elaine had never had a man look at her like this. As if he was seeing straight through her, with all of his desire reflected in his eyes. Desire for her. She was momentarily immobilized by the flash of attraction that raced through her. She'd never felt anything like the fluttering, twisting sensation that was curling low in her belly.

"What if I told you that I wanted you?"

She realized that she was starting to lean towards him, her lips parting slightly, as if in invitation, her eyes drifting closed…

She backed away from his touch as if she'd been burned, mortified heat flooding her face again.

"No! No. No. I mean, this is a business deal, and I've no desire to…muddy the waters by introducing anything physical, and anyway it's…it would be inappropriate." Her face was burning, and she knew she was glowing like a beacon. She was starting to wish she hadn't come. She was totally and completely out of her depth with him.

He laughed. She was absolutely priceless, clinging to her prim and proper persona. "Point taken."

It would be better that way. Much better to keep business and pleasure firmly separated. Especially when there was a marriage license involved. He didn't want to be tied to one woman for a year, and he had a feeling that if he did sleep with her, the "anyone at any time" offer would be revoked.

And anyway, if he changed his mind he could have her if he wanted her. He had seen it in her eyes, in the rapid beat of her pulse at the base of her elegant neck. She wasn't immune to him. But in his experience very few women were. They loved his status, his wealth, and his skill in the bedroom. Sometimes they even loved him. But *he* didn't love *them*. Ever.

"You would have to move into my penthouse," he said.

"Absolutely not!" And there it was again, that flustered look that made her seem soft, maybe even feminine. That made her seem so desirable.

He took a step toward her. "I can't exactly have my new wife living across town. I do have a reputation, after all. Any woman of mine is always kept as close as possible."

The low, seductive timbre of his voice caused a shiver to race up her spine. When she'd imagined this little arrangement she hadn't pictured them living together, somehow. The thought of being in such close quarters with a man as…disturbing as Marco made her feel…hot.

But she could do it. To get the business she would do anything. She wasn't about to let her life's ambition go. She would find the whole thing much more tenable if she brought him to her turf. Really, she'd find the whole thing much more tenable if he was living on another continent, but as that wasn't an option… "If we have to live together, *you* can move in with *me*."

"No," he countered, "*you* will move in with *me*." Poor Elaine. She really was so painfully naive. The first rule in a business dealing was to know your adversary. And she clearly didn't know him. Marco De Luca did not negotiate. "And you'll take my name."

"What?" Her face was red again, but this time he was fairly certain it wasn't from embarrassment. "I wouldn't do that if I was entering into a *real* marriage with you! It's anti-feminist! Making a woman lose her identity just because she's getting married! It's an archaic form of control!"

He shrugged. "So call me a caveman, then. I'm not exactly a modern, sensitive male. And the closest I get to 'enlightened' is ordering a latte. When it comes to relationships, just like in business, I'm in charge. No one would believe it if *I* moved in with *you* and you kept your maiden name. My distinguished conservative clients would lose a lot of respect for me if I let my little wife run rough-shod over me in her ugly clogs."

She curled her toes inside her sensible footwear, hating him for making her feel self-conscious about her appearance. She had made the decision a long time ago, and with good reason, not to put emphasis on her looks—in fact, she did the opposite. And she refused to be made to feel silly for wanting to be taken seriously based on her qualifications instead of how sexy her legs looked in heels and a mini-skirt!

"Fine," she said through clenched teeth.

"And—" his lip curled into sneer "—I expect you to understand that as my wife my satisfaction is your priority. I am expecting to take full advantage of all of the perks this arrangement can afford me."

Her mouth dropped open. "I told you I'm not sleeping with you. Don't you dare make me sound like a…a…*prostitute!*" She clamped her mouth shut again, her pulse pounding in her ears. The absolute rank arrogance of the man!

He barked out a laugh. "That isn't what I said. I won't have any trouble finding a woman to share my bed. What I need is a woman to hold on to my arm and gaze at me adoringly during business functions. When I have an engagement that requires your presence, it takes priority. Not your work. Not your social life."

He could see the internal argument she was having with herself play out in her blue eyes. "Fine. I agree to your terms."

He gave her a hard look. "There is no chance that I might be tempted to make this arrangement permanent. That isn't how I operate. Even if you do wind up in my bed, it will only be until I'm finished with you. Don't fall in love with me, because I certainly won't be falling in love with you." It was a slightly more blunt version of the standard disclaimer he presented at the beginning of every relationship. If there was one thing he hated it was a woman getting overemotional and acting shocked when it was obviously time to end the relationship. And relationships always had to end.

"I'll try," Elaine said dryly. She was grateful for that little slap back to reality. He was a domineering womanizer, the sort of man she despised. And she'd do well to remember that.

Don't fall in love with him? She nearly laughed out loud. She wasn't even sure she liked him. And anyway, how could you fall in love if you'd written off the entire emotion?

"Plenty of women before you have fallen for me. Or my wallet, whichever the case may be."

"Trust me when I tell you I'm not interested in your heart or your wallet. I'm fully capable of supporting myself financially, and as for my taste in men…well, it doesn't run toward relics from bygone eras."

A slow smile spread across his face. "We have a deal," he said.

She stuck out her hand and he shook it in mild amusement. The woman was all business. Except when she blushed.

"Well, Mr. De Luca, it will be a pleasure working with you." The professional smile she had entered with was pasted firmly back into place. "I'll have my lawyer contact yours, and they can begin drafting the prenuptial agreement. Send me a copy of your calendar so that we can make a decision on the wedding date."

"Of course," he said. She turned to go, her pants tightening against her pert, rounded backside as she strode to the door. "Ms. Chapman?" She stopped and turned to face him again. "I'll pick you up tomorrow at eight. We're going to go shopping for an engagement ring in the morning."

She looked as if she wanted to say something. Her lips quivered, then hardened, but she remained silent.

"Oh, and be sure to wear something…feminine."

CHAPTER TWO

ELAINE glared at her bedside clock as the shrill alarm reminded her that it was time to get out of bed. She hadn't slept at all. She'd just twisted around in a tangle of sheets, second-guessing everything that had taken place the previous day.

She was no romantic—far from it. She was a pragmatist right down to her ugly shoes. Marriage, at its heart, was only a business arrangement anyway. The signing of a contract to legally bind two people together, with certain penalties applying should the agreement be broken.

But suddenly it seemed so much bigger than just signing a contract. She was actually *marrying* the man.

She swung her legs over the side of her bed and padded over to her closet. Wear something feminine, he'd said. If only she didn't need his help so badly she would have told him exactly where he could stick his opinions on her style of dress. But she wasn't about to blow this deal by being stubborn over every small demand. She would save up for the big things. This, although a blow to her pride, she could do.

She rifled through the tightly packed closet. Nothing but severe-looking suits in dark colors. Practical, but not exactly pretty. Certainly not *feminine*.

Although his idea of feminine was probably a corset and fishnet stockings!

There was a pale yellow dress wadded up into a ball and stuffed in the far reaches of the closet. She picked it up and shook out the wrinkles. It had flowers. And it was a dress. That, she supposed, would qualify it as *feminine*.

She took a quick shower and shaved her legs hurriedly. She got out and propped her leg up on the vanity, dabbed at the razor cut on her knee, then made the fatal error of looking in the mirror. She grimaced at the face staring back at her. There were deep purple shadows under her eyes from lack of sleep. She looked like a raccoon.

It had been a long time since she'd tried to play up her looks. These days she took care to tone down her beauty by wearing suits that camouflaged her hourglass figure and by pulling her long golden hair into the tightest bun she could manage. She didn't like the way she looked, but at least it had made the guys at work stop patting her on the behind and sending her off to make coffee.

She looked at her make-up bag, shoved against the back of the vanity. It was actually dusty. She did a mental calculation on when she'd gone to her last charity ball. Six months ago. That was how long it had been since she'd touched make-up. But it was desperately needed now.

Even without the raccoon eyes she would feel inadequate enough on the arm of a man who looked like Marco De Luca.

He was the perfect example of how it was different for men and women in the workplace. Where his looks were an asset to him, hers made men treat her like their own personal Barbie doll and made women treat her as if she was the enemy.

In the beginning she hadn't disguised her body. She hadn't felt she was at a disadvantage being female. But she had learned very quickly. It had only taken one incident to have her blacklisted from every decent real estate firm in the city; one tiny rumor that everyone had believed without so much as a photo to confirm it.

Even the man involved in the incident had denied it, but that hadn't made a difference to any of the city's gossipmongers. In the end the man had been allowed to keep his job, and at the age of twenty she had learned exactly where she stood in the male-dominated corporate world.

She applied the bare minimum of make-up needed to cover up the dark circles, and put on a little blush, mascara and lipgloss to play up her features as subtly as possible. She was reasonably satisfied with the results. She wouldn't be winning any beauty pageants, but the make-up highlighted her features nicely, made them look softer.

She checked her bedside clock. She had five minutes. She raced to her dresser and sifted through her massive collection of underwear, pulling out a pale yellow lace bra and thong. Her affinity for girlie bras and panties was her one concession to femininity. And it was safe, because no one knew about it.

The doorbell rang, and the sound put an uncomfortable jittery sensation low in her belly. She clamped a hand to her stomach in an attempt the squelch the feeling. The last thing she needed was to start acting like a silly teenage girl with a crush. She hadn't acted like a silly teenage girl when she'd *been* a teenager. No reason to start now that she was nearly at the halfway mark of her twenties.

"Coming!" she shouted, still trying to clasp her bra.

She gave herself one last glance as she raced by the bedroom mirror, and grimaced. Her hair was starting to curl, and in no time it would turn into frizz. Normally she didn't dare let her hair dry naturally, but at the moment she didn't have time to worry about it.

She slipped the dress over her head as she hurried out of her bedroom. It was shorter than she remembered, ending above her knees, and the scoop neck showed a lot more cleavage than she remembered too. The last time she'd worn it had probably been her sophomore year of high school. But it was too late to change now.

She swung open the door and her heart slammed against her ribcage. If he'd been handsome yesterday in his suit, he was devastating today in dark blue jeans and white button-up shirt. The color of the shirt enhanced his golden-brown skin, and he had the sleeves scrunched up to his elbows revealing his muscled forearms.

That tightening sensation was back, winding through her midsection and sending electric pulses through her bloodstream. Muscled forearms were something else she liked, apparently.

She was staring. *Oh, no.* She was staring and she couldn't stop. Thankfully, he didn't notice. Or maybe he pretended not to. Or he was just so used to women gawping at him that he took it as his due.

"You're ready," he said, in a tone she wasn't certain was complimentary. He assessed her slowly, his brown eyes taking a leisurely tour of her body. She had to fight the urge to try and cover up. "Typical female behavior demands that you keep me waiting for at least half an hour."

"I haven't picked up my copy of *The Rules* lately, so I must be out of the loop," she said waspishly.

He chose to ignore her biting retort and let his eyes roam over her body again. "Don't you think it's a little chilly out for a dress that skimpy?" The dress ended well above her knees, showing off killer legs she'd done a great job of camouflaging with her baggy pants.

"Skimpy?" She tugged at the hem, as if trying to add length to it. "It's perfectly decent. Besides, it's all I had that was appropriately *feminine* for you." She said it sweetly, but he could feel her barely contained annoyance radiating off her in waves.

Fine. That made two of them. The last thing he wanted to do was take a woman shopping. Much less take a woman shopping for a ring. Commitment, and anything resembling it, had been something he'd always endeavored to avoid. He'd spent too much of his life looking out for the needs of others, being the stable influence. As soon as his younger brother had turned eighteen Marco had taken his life back, and he wasn't about to forfeit it again by thrusting into the claws of some greedy female.

Usually if he was going to buy a woman jewelry, or some other gift, he had his PA sort it out. Anything else was much too personal and might convey intent that was most definitely not there.

But this was a necessary evil. It would call attention to them. Give the press a bone to gnaw on. Which was exactly what he wanted.

"It's fine," he said, trying not to give away just how fine he thought the dress was. "Just get a jacket."

"Well, as long as it meets with your approval, Mr. De Luca." She grabbed a light jacket and swept out the door.

Marco walked behind her, trying not to pay too close attention to the sway of her hips and the flare of that dangerously short dress. He felt his body tighten and he nearly groaned out loud. Who knew that Elaine Chapman had been hiding legs that could bring a man to his knees? And that image brought to mind a host of interesting possibilities.

He pulled his keys out of his pocket and pressed a re-mote unlock button, making the headlights of a low-slung black Ferrari flash.

"I expected it to be red," she mused.

He chuckled. "I hate to be too obvious."

She had to bite back a laugh. Marco was completely obvious in every way. His clothing screamed wealth, from his custom-made suit jackets to his handcrafted Italian leather shoes. And his body screamed sex, from his broad shoulders to his bold swagger.

He wore his confidence with the ease of a second skin, and it made her envious. She doubted he did anything based on the approval or disapproval of others. He simply succeeded. He lived to please himself. She wanted that.

He opened the passenger door and gestured for her to get in. She stopped in her tracks and gave him a look that could have melted ice.

He quirked a dark eyebrow at her. "You don't allow men to open doors for you?"

"I can open my own doors." She was being pigheaded, and she knew it. She let men open doors for her all the time if they offered.

She saw a glint of something dangerous in his eyes. Something exciting. "Yes, I'm sure that you can. But as of today you are my woman. And that means that I will treat you as I would treat a lover, *bella mia*." He purred the endearment, and she felt it vibrate all the way down to her toes.

Her knees wobbled slightly and she gave in and sank into the car's plush leather seats to avoid giving herself away.

An arrogant grin lit his handsome features. "Now, let's go find you a ring. Something to show the world that you are mine."

* * *

When they entered Tiffany & Co. a thousand childhood dreams that she'd never actually had converged on her, and a wave of emotion swamped her. The sophisticated surroundings and the man standing next to her made for an intoxicating romantic fantasy.

"We have an appointment," he whispered, and placed his hand on the small of her back, guiding her past tall, elegant glass display cases filled with rows of sparkling, exquisitely designed jewels.

She could barely concentrate on the jewelry. All her concentration had gone to the spot where Marco's hand rested, low on her back. Other than the handshake, and when he'd tortured her with that soft, sensual brush against her cheek, this was the first physical contact she'd had with him. Actually, other than handshakes and the hand on her cheek, this was the first physical contact she'd had in a long time. She hadn't realized how starving she was for it.

A tall, spindly saleswoman moved from behind one of the counters and greeted Marco with a double kiss on the cheek. "Ah, Mr. De Luca. We have the private viewing room open for you. If there's anything particular you have in mind, you need only to ask," she said, in a French accent that Elaine assumed was fake.

Private room? "I don't need anything extravagant," Elaine protested.

"Nothing is too extravagant for you, *cara mia*." Marco's voice was so sticky sweet she was surprised it didn't rot his teeth.

The woman reached out and lifted up Elaine's hand. "Very nice fingers. Very slender," she remarked. "She should fit the sample size perfectly."

She was starting to feel as if both Marco and the twiggy saleslady saw her as nothing more than a living mannequin.

"This way." The woman gestured to a curved flight of stairs and led them into a chic, simply adorned room with sleek, modern furniture and a rich color palette.

A platter with fresh fruit and champagne had been laid out for them, and soft, soothing music was being piped in. Life was certainly different when you had billions of dollars at your disposal.

The woman went over to the streamlined desk and unlocked a drawer. She pulled out a cream-colored velvet tray filled with sparkling gems. "These are from our Signature collection. For the woman who wants to stand out."

The rings were all so large, so ornate. They were beautiful, but the idea of choosing one of these special rings for this…this fraud seemed wrong somehow.

"I don't know…"

"This one." Marco picked up an antique-style ring with a startlingly blue square-cut diamond in the center. "It would be perfect."

She pasted a smile on her face. So the offer of *carte blanche* really meant she got whatever he wanted. A ring that size was the equivalent of an animal marking its territory. Really, he might as well just skip the ring and tattoo the word "mine" on her forehead.

"Yes, but you know me," she said through gritted teeth. "I really do hate to be too obvious." She repeated his earlier words back to him.

She scanned the tray, looking for something that wouldn't make such a bold statement. Her breath literally caught when she saw the delicate emerald and platinum ring nestled in the bottom corner. Diamonds wove around the larger emeralds, giving it an old-fashioned, romantic feel.

The image that appeared in her mind of Marco slipping that ring onto her finger, his eyes full of some tender emotion she didn't recognize, caught her completely off guard.

Of all the times to romanticize!

He moved closer to her—so close that she could feel the heat radiating off his body. "That's the one you like?" His warm breath touched the back of her neck and made her stomach drop to her feet.

"I don't know." The thought of that perfect ring being a part of this sham almost made her feel sick.

"It seems very you. It's unique," he said, keeping his voice down to a husky whisper.

No wonder women fell at his feet. Everything about him was so dangerously seductive. She wanted so badly to buy into the fantasy. Just for a moment.

She closed her eyes. If she was honest with herself she knew she was never going to have a real wedding. Never going to experience this moment for real. Why not enjoy it?

"She would like this one, and a band to go with it," he told the saleswoman, not waiting for Elaine's response.

He was still standing too close, darn him! Her brain cells had gone on strike.

The woman went off to find a selection of wedding bands, leaving her alone with Marco. Her breath caught in her throat.

"Calm down," he whispered in her ear. "You're going to have to look like you enjoy my touch. Like it reminds you of pleasures we've recently shared." He ran his hand up from her waist to the underside of her breast. A tremor shot through her body and it made her shiver. She hadn't had this kind of contact *ever*.

He laughed low, his breath hot on her neck. "I don't think you'll have to *pretend* to like it."

His arrogant statement was enough to pull her out of her

sensual haze. She moved away from him, fighting hard to regain her sanity. She pretended to study one of the paintings on the wall, her body still tingling where his hand had made contact—and, more disturbingly, tingling in places he had *not* made contact.

The woman came back into the room with a simple platinum band, contoured to fit the asymmetrical design of the ring, in her hand. "This will be perfect."

"We'll have them wrapped, if you don't mind," Marco said, keeping his eyes trained on her. "I'm going to wait and present them to her later." The smile he gave her was so warm and intimate. And so not meant for her. It was for show. She didn't want to know what the cold, pressing sensation in her chest meant.

An hour later their purchases were wrapped up and they were back out in the morning sun, the warm rays banishing some of the chill that had been lingering in the air.

Marco's cellphone rang. "De Luca." He paused for a moment. "Yes. Go ahead and put me down for one hundred thousand." He paused again, and Elaine could hear a man's excited chatter on the other end. "Not at all. It's a worthy cause. Thank you. You too." He ended the call and put his phone back in his suit pocket.

"Was that for a charity?" she asked, feeling something soften inside her.

He nodded briskly. "A charity that provides financial support for the families of children with special needs. I make frequent donations to them."

"That's nice of you."

He stopped walking. "I'm not a nice man, *cara*. The sooner you realize that, the easier your life will be for the next twelve months."

"But you donated all that money…" She trailed off.

"And it benefits me. It will be a very high-profile donation. Philanthropy can be good for business." He turned away from her and started walking again, his strides so long she had to take two to his every one.

All of the soft feelings vanished. She knew he was ruthless when it came to business. His reputation was legendary. The man who, ten years ago, had become the youngest billionaire in the world. The man who crushed competition without a hint of conscience. He was well known for destroying any obstacles in his way, regardless of the fallout to anyone else. The bottom line was king. Wasn't the fact that he'd agreed to a marriage with her to boost his profits ample proof of that? Of course she supposed, as the marriage was her idea, she fell into the same category.

His reputation with the opposite sex was just as legendary as his business acumen. A couple of years ago he'd broken up with an Italian supermodel and she'd sold her story to one of the gossip rags. She'd spilled a lot of shocking details, and ever since then he'd become serious tabloid fodder. Elaine doubted that even half of what the woman said about him was true, but what she knew for sure was that he managed to be photographed with a different beautiful woman on his arm every weekend.

She had come in prepared for that. Prepared for the fact that he was sexy and that his charm was lethal enough to affect most any woman. But she had underestimated him. She had assumed that, with her practiced indifference to the masculine gender, she would be immune. The stark reality was that she was not.

It was the only downside to their little arrangement. She'd known he was handsome, she'd seen him at charity balls, around her father's office and in grainy magazine pictures, but she hadn't been prepared for how amazingly attractive he was up close. His face was square and undeniably masculine, yet his eyes, for lack of a better word, were beautiful. They were rich chocolate-brown with golden green flecks, framed by a fringe of long dark lashes. It was enough to make her mouth water. His body was another problem altogether.

She slowed her pace a little and allowed herself to take in the view. A frisson of something new and scary shivered through her. He had a broad, well-muscled chest that tapered down to a lean waist and narrow hips that led to— heaven help her, but she *had* noticed—the most heart-stoppingly sexy backside she'd ever seen. And she'd made those observations when he was fully dressed. If she lived with him, the odds of catching him without a shirt or— the image made her knees quake—in a towel were overwhelming.

He turned and quirked a black eyebrow at her, the glint in his eye letting her know that he was well aware that she'd been taking advantage of her position by checking out his assets.

She quickened her pace so that she was beside him again, the distracting view, as well as her erotic thoughts, placed out of sight. "Well, aren't you the master of the public image? A fiancée and a large charitable donation all in one day!" she returned tartly, banishing the images that were parading through her mind's eye.

"That's half of doing business, Elaine. You should know all about that."

Angry color rose in her cheeks. Leave it to this arrogant, infuriating man to remind her of her own personal black moment. "I do. I'm just not accustomed to seeing a public image that's so well crafted and so far removed from the true individual."

"Image is half, but business acumen and unflinching ruthlessness make up the rest."

She felt as if his dark eyes were looking into her, as though he could see through her polished, smooth façade, to the insecure girl inside her. She didn't like it.

"You have the ruthlessness, and a mercenary streak a mile wide. Selling yourself to me proves that."

Heat spiked through her. "I did not sell myself to you. Don't make me sound like a harem girl. I made a business deal with you. Yes, I used unconventional means, but there was no other way. Believe me, if there had been I would not be standing here with you."

"You misunderstand, *cara mia*. I admire your ability to shut off all of your finer feminine emotions in favor of marrying for mutual gain." He jerked open the passenger door of his car, which was parked closely to the curb. "So long as you remember that all you'll be getting out of this is your father's company."

He dipped his head close to her, his dark eyes blazing. She smelled the clean, musky scent of his aftershave and it made her stomach feel as if it had inverted.

She swallowed. "As I've already assured you, I have no interest in a husband. Nor do I have any interest in your vast fortune. I want what belongs to me. As my father's only child, I don't think it's outrageous for me to expect to inherit the company. I know I can do it, and if he would give me a chance he would know it too."

"Is that what all this is about? Proving yourself to your father?"

She ground her teeth together. "No. I want to take

control of my life and make something of myself. Surely you can understand that."

She sank into the car and he slammed the door behind her. He got in and turned the key aggressively, the engine of the car purring like a big exotic cat. "I'm a self-made man. Whatever I have I've worked for." He shifted into second gear as he eased into traffic and the engine growled as if emphasizing his point. "Including my reputation. A solid reputation is difficult to build, and one indiscretion can undo decades of work. That's why image is so important. I'm sorry if you find it duplicitous." His tone made it perfectly clear that he wasn't sorry in the least.

"It's why you need a wife," she said, trying not to sound smug.

He laughed—a low, dark sound. "I don't *need* you, *cara*, but I will certainly find use for you." He flicked an unconcerned glance at his wristwatch—a watch that undoubtedly cost more than her annual salary. "I have an appointment this evening that I cannot break." He turned to look at her, his dark eyes heating her, filling her with a longing that was nearly unbearable. "But you and I have a date tomorrow night."

CHAPTER THREE

THE phone had been ringing all day. How reporters had gotten hold of the extension to access his office line, he didn't know. Once the phone stopped ringing he would have to interrogate his staff.

Granted, he wanted press. That was the point of the arrangement. But he certainly didn't want the paps to have *personal* access to him. It was his PA's job to field phone calls, and he paid her handsomely for it.

The trip to Tiffany's had done its job, just as he'd planned. The picture of Elaine and himself entering Tiffany's together, and exiting holding the telltale robin's-egg-blue bags, had spawned a host of articles in every news source from the *New York Times* to *TMZ*—the latter speculating that it was a Mafia arrangement. His Italian heritage was all he could credit for the creation of that rumor. But then, when did a tabloid need anything silly like facts to come up with a story?

That, combined with strategically leaked information about his reservations at La Paz, a trendy restaurant in Manhattan, had the press engaged in a feeding frenzy to extract more information about Marco De Luca and his mystery woman.

He answered the phone midway through the first ring. "I'll tell you the same thing I've told everyone else. Ms. Chapman and I will comment when there is something to comment about." Denial, in his experience, was the best way to fuel a rumor. The more he downplayed it, the more interest would be piqued.

"That's a shame. I thought you'd be a little more straightforward with your own brother."

"Rafael." He was pleasantly surprised to hear his younger brother's voice. Despite living less than half an hour from each other, with Marco being a workaholic and Rafael being a family man, it was hard for their schedules to coincide. "I take it you picked up the paper this morning?"

"Actually, Sarah showed me. She loves all forms of gossip media. Though I doubt you're getting married to this woman to save her father from a mob hit."

Marco laughed. "Not even close. The Mafia has recently quit asking my opinion on whose knees they should break."

"Why *are* you getting married, then?"

Marco picked up a pen and started doodling on his day planner. "Oh, the usual reasons."

"Love?" Rafael asked, in what Marco thought was a hopeful tone. His brother had drunk the love Kool-aid a couple of years ago, and seemed to think that he should want to do the same.

"No. Financial gain." He explained how the arrangement had come about.

"Well, that sounds typically you," Rafael grumbled.

"That's because it *is* typically me, little brother. We can't all be happy running a dinky little real estate office. Some of us have ambition."

"My 'dinky little office' is a multi-million-dollar operation. And anyway, I have a wife I like to go home to every night."

Marco cut him off. "Well, that's fine for you. But I've raised one kid already, and I'm not planning on willingly doing anything like it again. Commitment of any kind is not on the agenda. This is for business."

Rafael cleared his throat. "I know that taking care of me wasn't easy. But I'm grateful for it."

"I don't need your gratitude, Rafael. You're my brother and I did it gladly. But this marriage, if you want to call it that, is strictly a business arrangement. The length of the marriage isn't indefinite. The longest it will last is a year. If neither of us has achieved our goal by then, we'll go our separate ways—no harm, no foul."

"And the woman? She knows that you're not madly in love with her?"

Marco huffed out a laugh. "I'm a ruthless bastard, Rafael, but not even I'm that bad."

Rafael sighed. "You're going to go ahead with this no matter what I say, aren't you?"

"Always. But you will agree to be my best man? It's the only chance you'll have."

"Of course I will. No one else would do it."

Marco barked out a laugh. "That's probably true. Now, let me get back to work, little brother. Some of us work for a living."

Marco turned back to his computer and tried to get on with his work day. The phone rang again.

The phone in Elaine's workspace rang for what seemed like the twentieth time since she'd come back from lunch.

She looked at it dubiously. It was either a reporter or,

worse, her father again. He'd called her at work early this morning, beside himself with glee that Elaine had managed to snare herself such a rich husband, and even happier that Elaine was finally settling down. Probably because her marriage, especially such a suitable one, would go a long way in blotting out that "unfortunate incident" from a few years back.

Thankfully he didn't seem suspicious about her marrying the man who'd just bought his company. He was too busy congratulating himself for raising a daughter who had finally wised up to the fact that a woman's place was in the home, not behind an executive's desk. And probably too confident in his skills as a businessman to even begin to think that his *daughter* could have seen a loophole that he hadn't.

She had ended the conversation with her father feeling renewed determination. That was exactly the reminder she'd needed for why this was necessary.

She picked up the phone. "Hello?" she said curtly.

It was another reporter, rattling off questions at lightning speed that were both personal and degrading. She hung up on the man mid-sentence, and rested her forehead on the cool veneer surface of her desk.

Her head popped up when she heard a knock on her office door—or, to be more accurate, her cubicle wall.

Marco's handsome face appeared around the corner, followed by the rest of him. Her mouth went dry at the sight of him. Her memories of how gorgeous he was didn't do him justice. And it had barely been twenty-four hours since she'd last seen him.

"Have the press been hounding you?"

She blew out a breath. "Yes. My phone has been ringing all day."

"The cost of doing business."

"So it seems." She sighed. "You know, I'm not putting myself through this just because I feel some sort of sense of entitlement—like I deserve it because I'm my father's daughter." It seemed important somehow that she tell him the details to make sure he understood what she'd accomplished and why she felt the way she did. She shouldn't care what he thought, but even as she reminded herself of that, she did care. "Four years ago Chapman's nearly declared bankruptcy. I identified a flaw in the system and helped my father rework the way products were shipped. It shaved four points off the cost and brought the company back into the black. I proved myself. I saved the company. My *family's* company. And still he'd rather let your corporation absorb what he built up from nothing than give it to me. All because I'm a woman. Do you see why I feel the way I do?"

"If everything goes according to plan, you should be getting exactly what you're entitled to." Truth be told, Marco wasn't the most modern guy. He was of the opinion that in general women should stay home and take care of their kids. But he could understand why she wanted to claim what was rightfully hers. It was a feeling he understood very well.

"Well, Miss Chapman." He took her hand and pulled her from her sitting position. "I believe you and I have a date."

"I'll just pop in and change. You can wait in the living room." Almost as soon as Elaine closed the front door to her apartment someone knocked on it. She opened it to a woman with spiky pink hair and a man whose eyebrows were more immaculately groomed than her own. "Can I help you?"

"I'm not sure how to say this tactfully, so I won't bother.

You need some help if you're going to look believable as my fiancée," Marco said from behind her.

Elaine stared blankly at him, the realization of what his statement meant slowly dawning. "You're giving me a makeover?"

"I'm not; they are." He gestured to the two people still standing at the threshold.

Her ears were burning. *A makeover!* "I'm not your dress-up doll, De Luca. You can't just mandate things like this!"

He sighed in exasperation. Why was *he* exasperated? She was pretty sure she ought to have the market on exasperation cornered at that moment.

"Why bother to fight me on this? You need it—trust me—and I'm going to get my way, so you might as well sit your cute little butt down."

She gave an indignant squeak and stood facing him with her mouth open.

"What? No snappy comeback?" he mocked. "I think I should notify the press."

She could not remember ever being so angry before. He was taking control from her bit by bit, and there was nothing that threw her off more than losing control.

She gave him a look that would have cowed most men. Leave it to her to get engaged to the one man who didn't seem to find her the least bit intimidating. "The measure of a woman is not her looks."

"Very nice sentiment. It's also patently untrue."

"It is not!" Great. Now he had reduced her to petty playground tactics.

"It most certainly is. And the same is true for a man. If you dress the part you'll be more likely to get the part. If I showed up at a board meeting in swimming trunks I wouldn't be taken seriously, and your feeble, stereotyped sense of style is hardly going to earn you any respect."

Neither had dressing feminine, but she certainly wasn't going to get into *that* with him. "Be that as it may," she said crisply, "I'm not here to play trophy wife."

He continued to smile for the benefit of the stylists, who were busy pretending to ignore the fight. She wasn't fooled by the grin frozen on his face. It had hardened, and his jaw shifted, the muscles in his shoulders bunched tight. "You're here to be whatever I ask you to be. And if I ask you to be my trophy then that's what you'll be. We *do* both want this marriage, don't we...*cara mia*?" The threat was implicit.

Icy fingers wrapped around her heart. She couldn't lose this deal. She had worked too hard. And she certainly wasn't going to lose it over something as trivial as a hair-trim and a little lipgloss.

She sat in the chair that was moved for her, keeping her face carefully neutral.

The petite hairdresser talked animatedly while she worked, waving her scissors every now and then to emphasize her point. She put a row of foils on the top of Elaine's hair, turning it a lighter, less brassy shade, and cut six inches off the length, bringing it up so that it just skimmed her collarbone, and added long layers to give it body and movement.

The man, Giorgio, was there for make-up and, Elaine wasn't terribly surprised to hear, eyebrow waxing. Her face was scrubbed and peeled and waxed and finally painted.

Giorgio stepped back and examined her like an artist looking at his masterpiece.

"I'm brilliant," he said as he handed her a mirror.

She barely recognized the woman looking back at her. She had fun, modern hair that looked full and healthy. Her face glowed, probably from the gold powder that Giorgio had brushed all over it, and her eyes looked larger and brighter with the expertly applied eyeshadow and her newly shaped brows. She hated so much to admit that it was an improvement. But it was.

Marco took her by the hand and pulled her up out of the chair, and dropped a light kiss on the tips of her fingers. Her legs wobbled.

"You look beautiful."

A new knock on her door broke the moment, and Elaine wrenched her hand from his. "I assume you know who that is too?"

He nodded, and walked to the door and opened it, taking a garment bag and tipping whoever it was that had made the delivery. "Your dress for dinner."

He placed the hanger in her hand, and she stared at it. He was changing everything about her, from her hair to her wardrobe, in order to make her look like his type. Either that or he was just trying to drive her insane.

She opened her mouth to offer up a sour comment, but the frosty look in his deep chocolate eyes stopped her cold. This was her end of the bargain—the part she had to keep in order to get what she wanted. She swallowed the comeback and went to her room, making her footsteps heavier than necessary, and unzipped the garment bag, revealing a filmy golden-brown dress with beaded spaghetti straps.

It fit her perfectly. *Too* perfectly. The gown clung to her curves like a second skin, showcasing her small waist and full bust, and revealing a little too much cleavage for her comfort.

Marco hadn't even asked her size. He'd guessed. If there was a more potent reminder of just how much of a womanizer he was, she couldn't think of it. And what was even worse was that she had a sneaking suspicion that the boiling feeling she got in her tummy when she thought about him with other women just might be jealousy. Which was a completely futile road to walk down. Men like Marco De Luca could have, and *did* have, any woman they wanted. And women like her were not exactly the women that men like him wanted.

She exited her bedroom, fighting the desperate urge to cover up her exposed figure. There had been a time when she might have liked the dress, might have felt beautiful. Not anymore. Now she just felt exposed. And the heated look Marco was giving her did not help. He evaluated her slowly, his chocolate eyes slowly caressing her curves. Heat flared in the depths of his eyes and it made her insides tighten. It felt as though someone had reached inside her and stolen the air from her lungs.

"Almost perfect," he said, reaching into his jacket pocket and pulling out a slender velvet case. "I went back to Tiffany's today." He opened the case and revealed the most beautiful necklace she'd ever seen.

The chain was made up of gossamer strands of white gold gathered together by delicate round-cut diamonds. The center pendant was a showcase of delicate craftsmanship, with intricate winding vines of platinum, and a large, perfectly cut emerald at the center.

He moved behind her and swept her hair to the side, his warm fingertips brushing her nape, sending a shimmer of sparks through her. "You're a beautiful woman, Elaine. Truly beautiful." She sucked in a breath when the cold jewelry touched her skin, the pendant settling between her breasts. "Your power is in your beauty. You should use it. Not hide it."

Heat curled through her. Pleasure, she realized. She liked having him say she was beautiful. She liked feeling beautiful. And she wasn't sure how she felt about discovering that weakness.

He put his hands on her bare shoulders and turned her to face him. "Now you look like my fiancée."

It was one of Manhattan's trendiest nightspots. A Latin-fusion restaurant decorated with old-world South American art, mingled with the clean, sleek lines of modern design. The hostess led them to his personal table, which was situated by the wall of slanted windows, overlooking the brightly lit city streets. But tonight he didn't fully appreciate his surroundings.

His thoughts were completely occupied with the woman walking next to him. He had thought the makeover would be helpful, but he'd had no idea that she would be transformed into a supermodel. No, not a supermodel. There was nothing angular or androgynous about her. She was all soft, curvy woman. Her looks weren't cookie cutter, or trendy. She was classic. Her perfect bone structure gave her the kind of beauty that not even age would diminish.

He'd thought she had a beautiful face when it wasn't enhanced with make-up, but with the subtle colors playing up her eyes and making them sparkle, making her lips look fuller and more inviting, she was stunning. One of the most beautiful women he'd ever seen.

Her hair, which he'd only ever seen in that schoolmarm bun or hanging wet down her back, was styled into soft blond waves that fell down past her shoulders and ended right above the swell of her lush breasts. And that necklace fitted right in the dip of her cleavage, touching her where he wanted to touch her.

This was the woman he had heard about. The one who could drive a man to do something stupid and reckless and condemn the consequences to hell.

And she didn't want to consummate their marriage.

He ran his hand down the length of her arm and moved it to the small of her back; he saw her pulse jump at the base of her neck. He fought the smug smile that tugged at the corners of his mouth. So she wasn't as unaffected by him as she wanted him to believe.

He pulled her chair out for her, and for once she simply accepted his offer.

She sat ramrod-straight, a strained look written across her delicate features. He reached across the table and took her hand, rubbing his thumb across the pulse of her wrist. "Do you ever relax?"

"No. Do you?" Her heart fluttered rapidly in her chest and a knot of excitement coiled in her stomach.

He leaned his head in so that his nose was nearly touching hers, and her fluttering heart stopped for a moment. "Only when I'm with a beautiful woman."

The intimacy of the moment was shattered by a flash-bulb that momentarily blinded her. She looked and saw a photographer sitting at the bar, trying to look nonchalant as he sat and drank his beer. "Is it always like this for you?"

He gave the photographer a sideways glance. "Not always, but being spotted together two days in a row is bound to have the paparazzi descending in droves. The prospect of me settling down has them chomping at the bit to get the scoop."

"I guess it's a good thing." Another flashbulb went off. Elaine's head whipped in the direction of the light. "We do want the word to get out."

She tried to feign indifference at the constant flashes punctuating their conversation, but it was almost impossible when she felt as if she was an actor in a play. Being on show was getting tedious, and it had only just begun.

By the time dessert arrived they had engaged only in small talk, and made no mention at all about the impending nuptials. It was starting to make her nervous. She knew he hadn't brought her here to discuss how well the Knicks were playing this season. Marco De Luca didn't do anything without a purpose. She didn't like feeling like this: unprepared, out of the loop. She had intended on retaining control of the deal, but he was wresting it away from her inch by inch.

Before she could take a bite of her tamarind white chocolate mousse, Marco stood and grasped her hand, then pulled her up so she was standing beside him. She had been afraid he was going to do something like this.

"Can I have everyone's attention?"

Elaine's heart rate kicked into overdrive. Oh, he was *not* doing what she thought he was doing.

"I have something I would like to ask this beautiful lady."

Yes, he was.

The press started snapping pictures like mad. It was the reminder she needed to try and look happy. She didn't need to try and look surprised.

"Elaine Chapman." He turned and looked her in the eyes, covering both of her hands with his. "Would you do me the honor of becoming my wife?"

He pulled out a small velvet box, and even though she knew exactly what was in it everything in her tightened up. She couldn't breathe properly. He opened the box and held the ring out to her. She stood frozen, unable to get a word out around the lump of emotion that was blocking her throat. She could only nod. He gave her a smile that stopped her heart; he looked like a man who had just proposed to the love of his life.

He slipped the brilliant ring onto her finger, and in that moment she could almost believe that he wanted her—almost believe that all of this was real. She felt tears sting the backs of her eyes, because she knew this moment would never be real. Not for her.

The people in the restaurant started to clap. Her knees started to buckle. Marco put his arms around her and pulled her up against him, bringing her flush against his hard body, and then he lowered his head and covered her mouth with his.

She stood completely still for a moment, so shocked she couldn't respond. Then he changed the angle of his head and teased her lips open with his tongue. She whimpered and wrapped her arms around his neck. His lips were soft and firm and she didn't care that the moment was being caught on film by a hundred cameras. She didn't care that they were in the middle of the restaurant. The only thing that mattered was this.

It had been so long since she'd been kissed. Years. But she couldn't think clearly enough to figure out how many. And she'd never been kissed like this.

He ran his fingertips down the length of her spine and she tangled her fingers in his thick black hair. She felt as if she was going to melt into a puddle at his feet. His tongue swept across her bottom lip and she abandoned all her reason to revel in the moment.

She thrust her tongue into his mouth and felt his body jolt. He anchored his hands on her hips. Her breasts felt heavy and an unfamiliar ache started to throb between her thighs.

Then he released her, and she wanted to grab his head

and pull him back to her regardless of the fact that they had an audience.

He smiled at her and leaned in to whisper in her ear, "I think that looked pretty convincing, don't you?"

The high she'd felt when his lips had touched hers crashed. It was all for show.

And as the flashes continued to go off, and people continued to clap, she stood with a smile fixed on her face and all she wanted to do was go home, crawl into her bed, and cry.

CHAPTER FOUR

"I CAME over so we could discuss the terms and conditions." Marco swept past Elaine and entered her tiny apartment without waiting for an invite.

"I told you I would have my lawyer contact you." She didn't want Marco and his disturbing presence in her apartment. It was her sanctuary, her refuge from the frenetic pace of her life. Bringing him into it seemed wrong somehow. She hadn't seen him since their faux engagement had gone into effect. Hadn't seen him since that kiss.

"I assume you've had contracts drawn up?" he asked.

She glanced at her briefcase. "Yes." She'd had them drafted as soon as she'd found the loophole in her father's contracts.

He smiled sardonically. "It's necessary that we discuss precisely what each of us expects from this union before anyone signs anything."

"All right," she said slowly. She studied the layout of her shoebox apartment. Papers covered most surfaces. It was a very orderly mess; everything was stacked neatly and organized. The kitchen and living area served as her office, and since visitors were rare she usually left everything out rather than sticking it back into neat little folders.

"We can work at the coffee table." She gestured to the low table in the middle of the living room.

She bent and picked up a stack of documents and moved them to the large metal filing cabinet in the corner. When she turned, Marco was leafing through one of the binders she'd left on the table.

He looked up at her, his dark eyes keen. "Your business plan?" She nodded and watched, feeling tense for some reason, as he skimmed the pages. "You have some very good ideas," he said finally, setting the black book back in its spot.

A flush of pleasure crept through her traitorous body. "Yes. I think I can double the profits inside of two years just by implementing basic technologies. There haven't been a lot of advances at Chapman's in the past few years. My father isn't the most modern of men."

Marco gave her a wry smile. "So I gathered."

She rushed on as if he hadn't said anything, the fire and excitement burning in her now. "I want to set up a website with online ordering. I also think the way the warehouses and call centers are run could be streamlined for greater efficiency and lower operating costs."

Her heart was beating a little faster, as it always did when she talked about the company. The man sitting on her couch had nothing to do with it.

"Very good." To his credit he didn't sound surprised, but still it made her feel defensive.

"Thank you. I'm actually pretty smart, you know." She couldn't resist adding, "I graduated from high school two years early, and I was at the top of my class at Harvard."

"And look at all you have to show for it."

She narrowed her eyes. "Is that an insult?"

"Only if you're unhappy with what you have to show

for it." And, judging by his critical expression, he thought she should be.

"Hey! He tells jokes," she said balefully.

"I'd do a song and dance but…I know where my talents are best served."

"And, as you know, sticking to what you're good at is the key to success."

He nodded, his hard features serious. "That and perseverance."

She would be shocked if Marco De Luca had ever had to practice much perseverance. He seemed like the kind of man who'd had everything handed to him in life—mostly because she couldn't imagine that very many people were brave enough to deny him anything. And even if they were brave enough, he was a very charismatic man. He drew people to him. She was sure he was very good at getting what he wanted, using honey *or* vinegar.

"So, what is it that you hope to get from our arrangement?" Marco asked.

"I want exactly what I said upfront. I want my father's company. Nothing more or less."

"You're an ambitious woman, Elaine. I find it hard to believe that you would be content with just your father's company when you could try and obtain so much more."

"Why? You think because I'm a woman that my highest end goal is to just marry some rich guy and spend my days lunching and shopping? I respect myself far too much to have my happiness be determined by a husband or anyone else."

Her own mother had been pathetic that way. Chasing after men in an attempt to gain the attention of an indifferent husband, searching for some sort of acceptance and validation at the hands of others. Elaine was making her own way, her own success. She certainly wasn't going to become the kind of simpering female her mother had been.

She'd worked so hard to distance herself from that sort of behavior. Ironic that one small rumor about her and her direct supervisor at Stanley Winthrop had undone every ounce of her work. Marco had been right about reputations: they were difficult to build up but so very easy to tear down.

A snide comment made from a co-worker she'd dated briefly, who'd taken offense at the fact that she hadn't jumped at the chance to sleep with him, had spread amongst other jealous interns until it had somehow blossomed into its own entity. She'd been sick when it had finally reached her. The story was that she'd been having illicit sex with her very nice, very married boss. And the man who had relayed it to her had gleefully given her all the graphic details that he'd heard.

It had been indescribably painful, knowing that someone she'd cared about, someone she'd kissed, had said such awful things about her, had set out to ruin her because she wouldn't hop into bed with him. She'd avoided men since then. No dates. And she honestly hadn't had many before that. Which was why, at the ripe old age of twenty-four, she was still a virgin. Which was fine with her. Hormonal awakenings had kind of passed her over. Until recently.

Marco settled on the couch, his dark eyes trained on her. "Just as well that you feel that way, as I have no intention of being tied down by a wife. Not permanently, at least."

"At least we agree on that point." She had a feeling it might be their last agreement of the evening.

"And we need to agree on another one. You cannot get pregnant. If you do, you forfeit the company, and you can forget any sort of financial allowance from me. I don't want a wife, and I definitely don't want diaper duty."

She blinked, shocked by the words that had just come out of his mouth. "I thought we'd already established that I wasn't going anywhere near your bedroom during the course of this…this marriage. And, seeing as you and I both know it isn't the stork that brings babies, I think fatherhood is the last thing you have to worry about." She wrinkled her nose. "Well, the last thing you have to worry about with me. I can't comment on behalf of your other lady-friends."

"I always practice safe sex."

It was the absolute truth. Marco had no intention of becoming some woman's meal ticket for eighteen years, and he was totally scrupulous in his sexual practices for both the sake of his health and his checkbook. But that didn't mean that some of his mistresses hadn't tried to find a way around the precautions. He'd caught one woman with an open box of condoms and a needle, and he'd watched as she'd put a tiny puncture in each plastic packet before putting them neatly back into the box.

Then there had been the woman who'd tried to pass another man's baby off as his. Never mind that she'd been eight weeks along and he'd only known her for two.

He was well familiar with the female mind and how it worked. Financial security and wealth was the highest goal for the vast majority of the fairer sex. His own mother had prized it above everything, even her two children.

"Well, you won't be practicing any sort of sex with me," she said, twin spots of color high on her cheekbones.

Her prim exterior amused him—especially knowing what he did about her. She made for a very intriguing challenge.

"What exactly are your other *terms and conditions*?" she said tartly, as if reading the tenor of his thoughts.

"Simple. I'm only agreeing to this for the benefit of my company. I need to be sure that I'll be gaining much more than I would lose by forfeiting Chapman Electronics. That means I need you on call twenty-four hours a day, seven days a week."

Elaine didn't like the sound of that, although the odd fluttering in her stomach seemed to indicate otherwise. "What am I on call for?"

"Business functions, personal dinners. Whatever I might need my *wife* for."

"What about my job…my *life*?"

"I thought the company was the most important thing in your life."

Desire burned in her chest. Desire to prove herself to her father, to everyone. "It is."

"Then that means for the next twelve months I'm your number one priority. I'm in negotiations right now with James Preston. He's selling one of his resort properties in Hawaii, but he doesn't want to turn it over to someone who might turn his nice family vacation spot into some debauched spring break hangout."

"Which is why you *need* a wife," she said, feeling triumphant.

The corners of his sexy mouth twitched with humor. "It's why a wife will be useful to me, yes."

"So I'm supposed to be evidence of your transformation from playboy to doting husband?"

"Something like that."

Oddly, she felt a little indignant for Marco. His personal life had nothing to do with what a good businessman he was. Apparently not even men were exempt from the archaic viewpoints of others. Not that she condoned the way Marco treated women, but it was still separate from how he ran his business.

"So it seems like we need each other," she said.

"It isn't a necessity for me. I want the resort just as I want to experience a profit increase, but you're the only one who really *needs* this arrangement. Don't forget that."

"You mean I should remember that when you pull me out of work in the middle of the day and drag me off to some art gala at which you expect me to play trophy wife?"

A slow grin spread across his face. Her heart beat a little bit faster. "Something like that."

"*What* is *this*?" Elaine slapped the thick stack of documents onto Marco's pristine walnut desk.

He didn't look up from his computer screen. "The prenuptial agreement that my lawyer drafted. Or was that not made clear by the heading?"

"Oh, that was made perfectly clear. It's *this*." She picked the papers back up and rifled through them before setting them down again. "*This* is what I'm talking about!"

He flicked the offending lines a glance. "The infidelity clause?"

"Is that its official title?" She'd never been so angry in her entire life—and that included the day she'd confronted Daniel the Rat about the salacious rumors he'd spread about her. "If I have an affair I lose the company, yet there are absolutely no limitations imposed on *you*! It's a blatant, unrepentant double standard!"

His dark eyes collided with hers; the heat of his gaze warmed her whole body. Rage was coursing through her veins, nearly blinding her with a red mist, and still he was making her body tingle with anticipation for something she didn't even have a name for.

"If that's how you see it." He shrugged in a classically

Latin manner. "I see it as protecting my…" he looked her over her in a way that made her squirm "…assets."

She crossed her arms over her chest, trying to disguise her stinging nipples. "I'm not your asset! We are supposed to be a team!"

He stood and rounded the desk, the sheer height and breadth of him as awe inspiring as it was intimidating. "No, Ms. Chapman, we are not a team. Do I need to remind you, yet again, that I'm the dominant party here? That means that you will do as I say." He picked the prenuptial agreement up from his desk. "You will remain out of other men's beds for the duration of our marriage. If you need sex, you get it from me. If there's even a hint or rumor of impropriety on your part the company stays with the De Luca Corporation."

She tried to fight the hot tide of embarrassment that washed through her. What was it about this man that rattled her so? "And what about you? You're still free to do whatever you want?"

He nodded, his jaw fixed. "With whoever I want, as I recall."

"That is the most disgusting double standard I have ever heard! You didn't mention *this* a few days ago when we were discussing 'terms and conditions'."

"I'm simply covering every possible eventuality. I can't afford to have my wife seen with other men. In a real marriage it would never happen. No woman runs around on me. And I don't share."

"Then neither do I. Enjoy the next twelve months of celibacy."

"And you think you can resist me?"

She laughed. "No question."

He hauled her to him, pressing her breasts against the

muscled wall of his chest. "I don't believe that." His lips crashed down on hers, his tongue pushing past her lips and tangling with hers.

She couldn't resist. She didn't want to. She just wanted this moment, this heady, sensual moment, so far removed from her normal life.

He lowered his hands to her bottom and pulled her tightly against his body, pressing his erection against her belly. She gasped and moved against him, enjoying the electrifying sensations pulsing through her, exulting in the fact that he was as turned on as she was. That she had been the one to turn him on.

Her breasts ached for his touch, their shameless peaks announcing to him just how aroused she was. A pulse throbbed hard between her thighs. She wanted him. She wanted him to show her everything she'd never even cared to learn about. Everything she'd always steadfastly ignored about herself and about men.

She moved her hands over the muscles on his back, then around to his chest. He was so firm. So hot. So perfect. Just what a man should feel like. She wanted to feel his body without layers of clothing between them. She wanted….

She pulled away from him and jumped back as if she'd been burned. "I'm sorry," she said.

Her lips felt tight and swollen, her breathing was ragged, and she knew some of her hair had escaped the confines of her bun.

"There isn't anything to be sorry about. We're going to be married in two weeks' time. We might as well sleep together. It would add to the *convenience*."

It was the last part that kept her from saying yes. Without that scathing reminder that it would mean nothing to him she might have agreed. But there was no way she could view sex as casually as he did. She didn't have the experience or the sophistication to treat it as a recreational activity. Combined with the fact that she simply didn't have the time to devote to discovering her sexuality.

"I can't do that. I don't…I don't see sex as a *convenience*." She took a breath, trying to conjure up that steely businesswoman she knew lived inside her somewhere. "What I mean is, I don't sleep around."

Marco stared at her flushed face, her red lips, her eyes still dark from passion. She wanted him, even if she couldn't admit it yet. Or perhaps she was holding out until she felt it was most advantageous for her to give in. "That's fine. But the clause stays in. If you want sex, you get it from your husband."

She swallowed hard, trying to keep her face neutral. "I don't think I'll be wanting any in the near future."

He shrugged. "It's up to you. I don't have to coerce women into my bed."

That was the absolute truth. He couldn't remember the last time a woman had turned him down—if there had ever been a time. He didn't like it now. He liked it even less that his body seemed to have some sort of fixation on a woman who wasn't fixated on him. It must be the novelty of it. It was unusual for him to have to pursue a woman. They came to him—frequently and easily. If he didn't end up in bed with Elaine it would be easy enough to find someone else, seeing as there was nothing forbidding *him* from doing exactly that.

But the idea of Elaine being with another man while she was wearing his ring had made him see red. He had told the truth when he'd said he didn't share. And in his mind marriage, even one of convenience, made her his. Old-fashioned and unenlightened, yes, but there wasn't anything he could do about it.

"You have an appointment with a bridal gown designer tomorrow at nine."

"I have work," she said sharply.

"I don't care. The wedding takes priority right now."

She put her hands on her hips. "Is this how it's going to be, then? For the next twelve months you're going to treat me like your personal doll?"

Marco shrugged. He seemed entirely unaffected by the kiss, and with her heartbeat still going erratically it irritated her.

"If that's the way you want to look at it. Or you could simply view this as your newest job opportunity."

"You know, you have a real talent for making me sound like a call girl."

"And you have a real talent for wasting my time. If you want to see me, next time make an appointment."

She drew up to her full height, but was careful not to get too close to him again. Desire and anger were still struggling for pride of place inside her. "I am your fiancée."

"No. This is a business deal, as you're so fond of pointing out, which makes you one of my business partners. Which means you make an appointment like they all do."

She leaned all her weight onto one leg, pushed out her hip and settled her hand on it, in her best indignant pose. "And do you kiss all of your business partners the same way you did me?"

"If any of them looked like you, I might. As it is, I've never been tempted to try."

It was difficult to decide whether to embrace anger at

his sheer male arrogance, or enjoy the sneaky glow of feminine pleasure she got from his underhanded compliment. In the end, it was the anger that won out. "I see. So you decided that because I'm a woman you can just kiss me whenever you like?"

He moved toward her, his dark eyes blazing with fury and something more compelling. "No. I kissed you because I wanted to. And *you* wanted me to."

"Your ego is impressive." She took a step back. "I didn't want you to kiss me. As you mentioned, this is a business deal, and I never mix business with my personal life." At least she was certain she wouldn't if she *had* a personal life.

The mockery in his smile told her he didn't believe her for a moment. "I know that this is all an affront to your feminist sensibilities, but for the purposes of this deal I'm your boss. You will do as I say. You will sign the prenup, and you will meet with the wedding coordinator tomorrow morning to choose your wedding dress."

Everything in her raged out of control. Her hormones were still on red alert from the kiss, and her temper had just about reached its breaking point. She sucked in a calming breath. This was where years of training kicked in. Where she played the game. This was business. You fought the battles you could win, not the ones you were destined to lose.

"And will *you* be attending this bridal gown extravaganza?"

"Absolutely not. It's bad luck for the groom to see the gown before the wedding."

"I would imagine that it's bad luck for the marriage to have a predetermined end date," she returned crisply.

He acknowledged her comment with a slight smile, then turned, walked back to his desk and settled behind it. Apparently she was dismissed.

She turned to go.

"Elaine?"

She stopped at the sound of that sweet, honey-coated voice saying her name, sending waves of sensation through her body. Well, wasn't *she* one to dramatize?

"I hope you don't have plans tonight."

She turned and arched her eyebrow. "Would it matter if I did?"

"Certainly. I would feel bad for asking you to break them."

"You most *certainly* would not."

The left corner of his mouth lifted into a half-smile. "You're right. I wouldn't at all. I have a dinner party that I'm expected to attend tonight and I need a date."

"Did you misplace your little black book?"

He gave her a pained look. "I don't have a black book." He picked up his gleaming cellphone and waved it. "That would be old-fashioned."

She felt her lips thinning into an unattractive line. "You're straight out of the Dark Ages. A BlackBerry isn't going to fix that."

"Nice to know you hold me in such high regard, *cara*. Did you drive here?"

She eyed him warily. "No. I took a cab."

"Perfect. You can ride with me."

"And if I have plans?"

"Cancel them. As per our agreement," he said.

"As per your *demands*."

"If you like." He seemed completely unconcerned by her anger, which only fanned the flame. "But I can hardly show up at this dinner without my new, highly publicized fiancée."

"Just tell them your fiancée has a life, and doesn't just hang on your arm professionally twenty-four hours a day."

"Oh, they know you don't do that. I'm sure they think you spend at least twelve hours wrapped around me in bed."

She flushed, her vocal cords failing her. The images that were pinging through her brain were graphic, and much more intriguing than she'd like to admit.

She had done so well, burying any interest in the opposite sex beneath piles of ambition. Then she'd walked into Marco De Luca's office and her long-ignored hormones had sprung to life and hadn't left her alone since.

"In any case, I need you to play your part. This is business, remember?" He said the last part with a mocking edge to his voice.

"I won't forget."

The dinner party was hardly the intimate affair she'd imagined. There were at least two hundred of Manhattan's most elite social movers in attendance, and it made it hard for her not to be grateful for the dress Marco's efficient PA had provided for her at the last minute.

It was too short and too tight for her taste, but judging by the similarly bedecked Barbie dolls that were hanging on their date's arms the look was par for the course.

Marco gave the stunning, reed-slim hostess a kiss on both cheeks before putting his hand on Elaine's back and introducing her. "This is my fiancée, Elaine Chapman. Elaine, this is Caroline Vance. She's the chairperson of the De Luca House charity."

"Nice to meet you." She shook the other woman's perfectly manicured hand, and held back the questions that were forming in her mind. Marco had never mentioned that he had a charity, but his fiancée would certainly know all about it. Well, a real fiancée would at any rate. She was clueless.

"Nice to meet you too." Caroline smiled warmly. "I didn't think I'd live to see the day when Marco would settle down. He's always preferred life in the fast lane." She shot Marco a teasing look. "I guess you're merging into the carpool lane, huh?"

The smile on Marco's face looked forced to Elaine, but Caroline didn't seem to notice. "Yes. It was time. When I met Elaine I knew I couldn't let her get away."

"Welcome to the club. You'll enjoy it." She gave Marco's arm a squeeze.

Marco paused and pulled his checkbook from his pocket, and filled in an amount that made Elaine's eyes widen.

Caroline took the check from Marco's hand, a broad smile on her pretty face. "He's generous to a fault," she said, her comment directed at Elaine.

Elaine smiled back, hoping she didn't look as confused as she felt. "Yes, he is."

Marco chuckled darkly as Caroline fluttered off to greet the next couple that was entering the ballroom. He took her arm and led her to a cluster of tables that were designed with intimacy in mind. They were small—so small that when she took her seat and Marco took his their knees brushed beneath the table. Her heart sputtered.

"All of the food, and all the prep work that went into the food was donated," he explained. "The guests paid two hundred dollars for each plate. All of the proceeds will go to the De Luca House."

She smiled. "That's great. What is the charity for?"

A shadow passed over his face for a brief moment. "Homeless children. It's an issue that's close to my heart."

She realized at that moment just how little she knew about the man sitting across from her. His background wasn't exactly a mystery, but there hadn't been a lot of information on his childhood either. She'd found out through her careful research that his father had been a wealthy Sicilian businessman who had moved his family to New York when Marco had been a young teenager. But between that event and his meteoric rise to success in the real estate industry and beyond she hadn't been able to find any details about his life. She'd just assumed he'd been growing up. Now she wondered. Marco claimed he was a self-made man, which meant that he'd built his empire up without the aid of his father's riches.

She looked at him. He was engaged in a conversation with the couple next to them, his speech pattern eloquent, his manner perfect. His profile was aristocratic, and he wore tuxedos as though the whole concept of formalwear had been built around his physique. He didn't look like a man who had ever struggled for anything.

At that moment, though, no amount of research into his background could have prepared her for the very disturbing effect Marco was having on her. She could hardly taste the gourmet dinner that had been prepared for the evening. Every few minutes her knees would brush Marco's beneath the table, or someone would come to speak to Marco and congratulate them on their engagement, and Marco would take her hand and look lovingly into her eyes. Or, worse still, he would draw her hand to his lips and press a tender kiss to her knuckles and send the butterflies that had taken up residence in her stomach into tailspins.

When the plates were cleared, after-dinner drinks were served—which Elaine declined. Her defenses were weakened already. No sense at all throwing alcohol on the burning fire of her attraction to Marco. So instead she sat still in her chair, ramrod-straight, trying her best to smile at everyone who cast a glance in her direction, and trying not to jump a foot in the air every time Marco's leg made contact with hers.

Tinkling crystal distracted her, and Elaine looked across the room at Caroline, who was standing on a riser at the far end of the room.

Caroline cleared her throat and the hum of conversation diminished. "I'd like to thank everyone for coming this evening. Your support means a tremendous amount. And I'd like to introduce the founder of De Luca House—Mr. Marco De Luca."

Marco gave her a wry smile, stood from his seat and bent down to drop a lingering kiss on her cheek before he crossed the long expanse of the room. She couldn't help but notice the sheer masculine grace his movements possessed. He stepped on the stage, his magnetic presence drawing the attention of everyone in the room and holding them, spellbound, in the palm of his hand. Her included.

"Thank you all for being here." His rich velvet voice rolled over the room. Her stomach tightened. "In these economic times I know making large contributions might seem like a lot to ask. But I ask you to remember that these children have likely never had the most basic necessities, even in the best of times. They don't have food, or clothing, or even shelter. They give no thought to four-star restaurants when they would give anything for a loaf of bread. What does fashion mean to them when they don't have a coat to protect them from the elements?"

Elaine felt her throat constricting as she looked into his earnest dark eyes. Something near her heart shifted, and she wished more than anything that she could make it shift back. Because lust was bad enough, new enough, scary enough, without there being emotion involved.

Marco continued, his slight accent making his speech

all the more compelling. "And how can we be concerned about keeping our summer homes when they do not even have the bare minimum of shelter?"

His speech went on, his words impassioned. He cited heart-wrenching statistics about how many of New York's homeless were children who had fallen through the cracks in the system. The charity worked to provide those children with homes that would give them a sense of family, an education, and even occupational training. The vision was to provide them with a base they could always come back to, even after they reached legal age.

When Marco had finished, many of the guests were blinking back tears, and she had a feeling the emotions Marco had brought out in them would be reflected in their donations.

Marco made his way back to where she was standing, pausing at intervals to shake hands and direct people to the donation area.

When he came back to her side he wound his arm around her waist and her heart did a freefall into her stomach.

"That was…" she struggled to sound unaffected "…a very nice speech. I had no idea there was so much need."

His dark eyes were clouded. "Many people assume that the government is taking care of all of the displaced children, but that is not the case."

It hadn't been the case for him. He and Rafael had been abandoned—first by their father, then by their mother. And no one had stepped in. No one had known about the two young teenagers who had been left to fend for themselves.

"Many people are unaware of what goes on in their own backyard. I consider it my duty to educate them and to do what I can."

She chewed her lush bottom lip, and he had the strongest urge to use his tongue to soothe away the marks her teeth had left in the tender pink flesh. "So not all of the nice things you do are for public image?"

He chuckled darkly. "Not all. But most."

A pianist began to play a slow, jazzy song, and couples started to migrate to the dance floor. Her body language was screaming that she didn't want him to ask her to dance.

"Elaine, I think I should have this dance with my fiancée."

He was amused when she pressed her lips into a thin line, her tension palpable. What would it take to kiss those lips into soft, willing supplication?

She was the epitome of hot, sexy woman in the skin-tight black dress that showcased curves so tempting they would make a priest sin, and still she maintained that untouchable aura of hers that she always threw up like a shield unless he kissed her.

She looked at the people around them, as if evaluating the situation to see if she could get away with a refusal. "All right." She said it as though he'd offered her a jail sentence.

It was a source of fascination to him that this woman, who was so obviously attracted to him, so responsive to his touch, his kiss, acted as though physical contact between them was anathema to her.

Elaine tried to quiet the pounding of her pulse. She looked at the couples on the dance floor, their bodies entwined as they moved in a rhythm that seemed far too…sexual to simply call it dancing.

Marco trained his bright white smile on her, but this smile was different than any other he'd given her before. It was almost predatory. He extended his hand. "Dance with me."

Not a question, a command. And for some reason a thrill ran through her rather than the anger that she'd expected, *needed*. Something about him was breaching her defenses, softening her. He was surprising her. He wasn't just a shallow playboy, and she had been much more comfortable with him when she'd been able to just write him off as such.

She accepted his offered hand, hoping he didn't notice that her own was damp with perspiration, and allowed him to lead her onto the dance floor. *Not smart*. Her practical inner voice was all but screaming at her.

Necessary, she countered, ignoring the churning pleasure in her stomach when he took her in his arms and brought her close to the heat of his body. Dancing with her fiancé was necessary. It wasn't about anything but keeping her end of the bargain.

The music was sultry, captivating, and she found herself swaying in time to the rhythm. One of his hands held onto hers, the other was low on her back, holding her to him, bringing her breasts into contact with his hard muscled chest. Her nipples tightened, ached. It was so unfamiliar, unexpected, and no matter how much she wanted to she couldn't hate it. She couldn't even muster up a faint dislike for it.

Her heart was pounding and she was certain he must be able to feel it. Certain he would be able to see the fluttering pulse that she could feel moving at the base of her throat.

Marrying a stranger didn't frighten her. Standing up in front of family and friends making vows she wasn't going to keep didn't bother her in the least. The thought of running a company wasn't scary at all. Not next to this— this attraction that she didn't want or understand. She always had control, and this sudden absence of it was terrifying. And oddly exhilarating.

She gripped his broad shoulders more fiercely in an instinctive effort to keep her knees from buckling beneath her. She regretted that instinct almost immediately.

He chuckled low, his hot breath fanning across her cheek, his grasp becoming stronger. Everything in her suddenly wanted to lean into him, kiss him again, to feel his mouth, hot, hard and insistent on hers.

She pulled away from him, her breathing labored, her body sluggish from unfamiliar desire. He looked amused. It was infuriating. Even worse that he knew exactly how he had affected her.

"Why do you pull away from it, Elaine?" he asked, his dark eyes compelling. Tempting.

"From what?" Playing ignorant was pointless, and she knew it, but pride and a desperate need to gain some sort of control pushed her to try anyway.

"From this." He hooked his arm around her waist and drew her to him, tilting his hips so that she could feel the length of his hardened arousal.

She drew in a shaky breath. "Because I don't feel the same way."

He chuckled. "This isn't about feelings. This is about lust. Want. Need. And you *do* feel it." He stroked a thumb across her hot cheek. "It's written all over your pretty face."

And just like that he was back in the slot she'd placed him in at their first meeting. It was a relief. But it didn't cause her own arousal to lessen. Her breasts felt heavy, sensitive, and she felt an embarrassing slickness well up between her thighs. She didn't have to be an expert on sex to know that her body was getting ready to experience it.

Too bad.

"I'm not interested in getting played, Marco. When I proposed to you it was so I could have the company, not a fling." It took every ounce of willpower she possessed to make her voice even and steady.

"Elaine Chapman?" Elaine turned to face the source of the voice, and her stomach sank to her toes when she recognized the man who had spoken her name.

"Yes?" She tried to appear poised, blank. She had perfected the act over the past few years. Better to be seen as an ice queen than to be seen as a slut.

A sick sensation weighted down her stomach. Daniel Parker. The man who had ruined her reputation because she hadn't slept with him. She knew he wasn't going to pass up the opportunity to fling a few insults at her now.

She straightened her posture and mentally braced herself. It simply wasn't in her to shy away from a challenge. She would not allow this man to intimidate and demean her. He'd gotten away with it once; she wasn't letting it happen again.

Marco cupped her elbow and stuck his hand out toward the other man. "Marco De Luca. I'm Elaine's fiancée."

"Really?" Daniel drew the word out, extending it several syllables. He shifted his focus to Elaine. "Your taste in men hasn't changed, then."

She bit her tongue. She didn't want to have this conversation, now or ever. Living through the humiliation and condemnation, and her subsequent barring from every decent firm in the city, had been bad enough. Rehashing it now just seemed stupid—especially when the man in front of her seemed to be out for blood. In a very sophisticated way, of course. There was no other way amongst the Manhattan elite.

To Marco's credit, he didn't comment. To Daniel's discredit, he pressed. "You always did prefer a more powerful man."

"I just prefer a man with as much ambition as I have," she answered waspishly, tightening her hold on Marco's arm. The fresh scent of his aftershave tickled her nose and, along with the surge of anger, quickened her pulse. "And they're difficult to find."

Daniel's smile turned cruel. "I would have thought it would be difficult to climb the corporate ladder lying flat on your back."

Her face heated unbearably, and she felt a surge of adrenaline infuse her veins with trembling energy. From the curious and condescending glares the other guests were giving her she knew no one in the immediate vicinity had missed Daniel's sleazy allegations.

"At least I don't feel as though I have to step on others on my way to the top," she said coldly.

"Of course not, Elaine," Daniel said, his eyes glinting. "You've just had to straddle others on your way to the top."

Adrenaline surged through her, and she clenched her fists to try and still her shaking hands. Daniel didn't wait for a response from her; he simply took the arm of his graceful, cold-looking date and walked away from them.

Marco put a hand on her elbow. "Do you want to leave?"

She looked around the room. People were still staring. She set her jaw. "No."

He regarded her closely. "You look like you might break at any moment. I think for the sake of your pride it would be best if we left."

She swallowed the lump that was rising in her throat and nodded her consent. She wasn't going to cry, she wasn't a crier by nature, but there was a very real danger that she might end up dumping a drink on Daniel's head.

Marco thanked Caroline for hosting the event and

slipped his arm around Elaine's waist, leading her down to the limousine that was idling at the curb. He opened the door for her and she slid inside. He got in and sat beside her, sitting closer to her than was strictly necessary.

"Are you all right?" Marco asked, studying her drawn face. The encounter with that man had disturbed her. She had kept her wits in place, not letting him cow her, but it had affected her.

She angled her face away from him, keeping her eyes trained on the brightly lit streets. "Of course. People like that are a part of life, aren't they? People who resent the success of others."

"Perhaps just their methods," he said coolly.

"Perhaps. But if I really was climbing the corporate ladder I doubt I would be stuck in a cubicle."

"I doubt you would be stuck in a cubicle if you hadn't been caught messing around with your married supervisor. Word spreads."

Her head whipped around. "And sometimes word is wrong. I can't beat the rumors, Marco. Believe me, I've tried. No one believes the truth, and the lie makes me a liability that nobody wants around the office. So I've found my way around it. Hard work isn't going to be enough—not with all of that—" she gestured toward the direction of the hotel "—hanging over my head. But I'm not the woman Daniel says I am, and I refuse to be punished for sins I didn't commit."

Marco shrugged. "Frankly, I don't care what happened. Whether or not you slept with your boss is wholly irrelevant to me. But I must warn you that while some men might be easily blinded by generous curves, I'm not. You can't use your body to get to my heart or my bank account."

She clenched her teeth. "My body isn't on offer."

"Really?"

She was angry, he could see that, and it was genuine. At being called out or at being falsely accused, he wasn't certain. He knew she was calculating—he had known it before she'd walked into his office. But it was no matter to him. He was hardly going to become a victim of her machinations like her foolish supervisor had supposedly been. He wasn't going to be swayed by her tempting mouth and her lush curves. He was far too jaded for that.

Of course she was welcome to try. It would make the next twelve months interesting.

"Really," she stated emphatically. "For what it's worth, I have too much pride to seduce my boss into promoting me."

He studied the haughty tilt of her chin. It was very possible that she did have too much pride to do anything like that—now. She had been very young after all.

"It's no matter to me one way or the other."

She scoffed. "Not worried that I'll take advantage of you?"

"Not in the least." He had infinite experience with conniving women. "Although you're welcome to try."

Angry color suffused her milk-pale skin. "I don't think that will happen. We have a deal. I already have what I want," she said stiffly.

He moved his hand to her soft cheek, letting his finger drift along her silken skin. He felt a sharp tug in his midsection and his shaft hardened. What was it about this woman that made her such a temptation? "But what if you could get more? Doesn't that appeal to you?"

She blew out a breath, its heat fanning across his hand. "No. I only want what I earn."

A slow smile spread across his face. "That could be taken many different ways, *cara mia*."

"You know what I mean," she said tightly.

The limo pulled up at the curb in front of her small, shabby apartment building. Neither of them moved.

She parted her lips and slicked her tongue across their surface. She was pure temptation. And he wasn't used to resisting.

He leaned in, half expecting her to draw back. But she met him in the middle, her soft lips clinging, her mouth molding to his, her tongue testing him almost shyly. He cupped the back of her head and crushed her to him, delving deep inside her mouth, tasting her.

She pulled back abruptly, shoving hard at his chest, her blue eyes rounded, her lips pinched. "That shouldn't have happened."

"It was only a kiss," he growled, knowing he sounded as frustrated as he felt. But he had been ready to take her in the back seat of his car, with only the privacy shield and tinted glass between them and the world.

"And it shouldn't have happened," she insisted.

She ran her hands over her tightly knotted hair. Even after their passionate interlude there wasn't a lock out of place, he noticed with wry humor.

She drew in a sharp breath and thrust her chin high, her prim façade firmly back in its place. "I would invite you in," she said tartly, "but I don't want to."

"You want me to come in. You're just afraid of what might happen if I do."

She looked thoughtful. "You're right. This might be the perfect opportunity to seduce you out of your millions. But, darn it all, I have a headache."

He laughed. At least she was amusing. "I guess even temptresses need a night off now and then."

She gave him a humorless smile and stepped out of the car.

"Elaine?"

She paused, her expression cautious.

"Next time I see you you'll be wearing a white dress."

CHAPTER FIVE

THE wedding had become sort of much-anticipated society event, despite how little time had passed between the announcement and the actual ceremony—or maybe *because* of that reason. Elaine couldn't help but think that the haste of the marriage was part of what made it interesting.

She felt half the eyes in the historic church examining her flat stomach speculatively as she walked down the long aisle.

The air was heavy with the perfume of flowers, compliments of her overzealous wedding planner, and the late-afternoon sun streamed through a round stained glass window, throwing squares of blue light onto the stone floor. It was a beautiful wedding. But it was someone else's wedding. None of it was to her taste except for her simple dress. But none of that mattered. All that mattered was what would happen twelve months from this moment. When the company she had worked so hard for would be hers.

She raised her eyes and looked at her groom, waiting for her at the head of the aisle. She had never seen him look so handsome. His tuxedo was black and well fitted, showing off broad shoulders and a tapered waist. He was in fantastic shape, but hours in the gym weren't the biggest contributing factor to his immense appeal. He was handsome, criminally so, his chiseled features the perfect blend of masculinity and beauty. But it was his charisma, his raw confidence, his power that made people gravitate to him. He wasn't like any man, any person, she'd ever met. And she was about to marry him.

She swallowed. Her throat felt like the inside of a pincushion.

This is nothing but a business deal. Nothing but another contract.

She shifted her bouquet and took her groom's hand.

Elaine had no idea how she'd managed to make it through the ceremony, the receiving line, and four hours of the reception. Her feet hurt from wearing her extremely impractical shoes, and her face hurt from all the overly cheerful smiling. And dancing with Marco, clinging to his arm, trying to pretend that she wasn't melting from the heat he was making her feel, had been as taxing as it had been torturous.

She sank into the limo with a sigh, and rested her head on the back of the seat. "That was exhausting."

"New brides usually say that *after* the honeymoon."

Heat flooded her face. Her treacherous mind was all too willing to offer up possible ways Marco could tire her out. She did *not* need this. Not now, and not with this relic from the Dark Ages.

The limo, which had been decorated with over-the-top script writing that said "Mr. and Mrs. Marco De Luca", pulled up to the curb in front of Marco's penthouse. She didn't wait for him to open the door for her. She got out and waited for him by the entrance of the building.

He caught up to her and passed her by, his long legs

taking strides much faster than her own legs could carry her. She'd changed after the reception into a white silk pencil skirt and a green sweater, but she was still wearing the ridiculous stilettos, which made walking fast a little tricky.

She trailed after him down the long marble corridor. This was the sort of love den she'd expected a man like him to own. His women probably fawned over it. Then over him.

Her stomach lurched at the thought of him bringing other women back here. How many had there been? More importantly, how many would she have to see during their marriage? Would she be able to *hear* them as she lay in her own bedroom trying to sleep?

"This is my elevator."

"You have your own personal elevator?" All those little tarts he paraded though here probably *loved* that.

"Yes, it acts as the main door to my house. It would be a security risk if everyone could use it." He spoke to her as if she might be a small child.

"Does everyone have their own elevator?"

"No, just me." He offered a smug grin at that.

He entered a key code into the number pad that was on the lift and the doors opened. The ride up was a long one; he was on the top floor, naturally—what penthouse wasn't? When the ping signaled that they had reached their destination, the doors opened and revealed a bright, airy living room. It didn't match with the rest of the building at all. Nothing tacky or overdone about it. No gold filigree on the windows. No champagne glass hot tub dominating the room.

Far from any of the glittering garishness she'd imagined, it was a contemporary design with clean, sleek lines that didn't suffer from the impersonal, cold feeling of some modern décor.

White walls and vaulted ceilings added to the feeling of openness, along with floor-to-ceiling windows that afforded a fantastic view of the sparkling Manhattan skyline.

The kitchen and living room flowed into one another seamlessly. The countertops in the kitchen were granite, and the appliances were top-of-the-line stainless steel. It was a modern luxury Mecca. The kind of home she'd always imagined setting up for herself. Of course her over-crowded one-bedroom apartment with its mismatched sec-ondhand furniture could hardly compete with Marco's spacious, state-of-the-art penthouse. She just didn't have the cash to own such high-end things. Loath as she was to admit it, living here wasn't going to be a trial.

"You like it?" Marco asked. His husky, sexy voice sent a tremor through her body, and she had to tamp down the wave of longing that threatened to rise up and swamp her. No, it was going to be a trial, all right. Just a luxurious one.

"I do. It's very tastefully decorated, and the view is amazing. Although the windows don't offer much privacy, do they?"

"Will we be needing privacy?" He raised his eyebrows, his expression one of keen interest.

Her face went hot. "No! I just meant…I mean because people could see in."

"They can't. It's one way glass. But I'll make a mental note that you intend to do things in my living room that require privacy." He gave her a look that was so hot it nearly melted the soles of her ridiculous shoes. "I'll make it a point to work from my home office more often."

It was at times like this that she really wished she could come up with some witty, off-the-cuff remark, but his casual innuendos always left her a mess.

She cleared her throat and tried to salvage some dignity. "Where is my room?" Anything to escape.

"Down the hall, last door. You have your very own *en suite* bathroom, so you'll have all the *privacy* you need. I'll be in my office; I have some work to do." She didn't watch to see which direction he went—didn't even try to. She just headed down the hall, the promise of a hot bath keeping her going.

Her bedroom was white, like the rest of the house, and she was pleased to see that she had a view of the city skyline out of her window as well. It certainly beat the view from her own apartment, which consisted of a brick wall and her neighbor's bedroom window.

All of her worldly possessions, except for her furniture, had been brought over by movers earlier today, and most everything was still packed away in boxes and stacked neatly in the corner. She wrinkled her nose. She wasn't going to be unpacking tonight. All she wanted tonight was her bath and then bed. An image of Marco, his chest bare, his skin tan against her white sheets, flashed in her mind.

Alone. She would be going to bed *alone*.

She padded into the bathroom and her heart nearly stopped. There was a separate shower and jet tub, all tiled with caramel-colored Italian marble. The tub was so deep it looked as if she could sink in up to her neck and lose herself completely.

She went back into her bedroom and rummaged around until she found her iPod, then gave a casual scan for the bag she'd packed her clothes in. She didn't see it, and decided to forego searching for pajamas until after she'd had a chance to let the warm water work the knots out of her muscles.

It took a while to fill up the massive tub, but it was worth the wait. Elaine submerged herself in the warm water and felt the tension slowly recede from her tightened muscles. She laid her head back and closed her eyes, letting the events of the day slip from her cluttered mind.

Her quiet moment was shattered by a rush of cold air. She jerked her head up and scrambled to cover anything that might be showing when she saw Marco standing in the doorway.

"Good—glad to see you're making yourself at home."

"Get out!" She had never been naked in front of a man before. She very likely hadn't been naked in front of anyone since she'd been in diapers. She was the type to avoid public locker rooms and showers.

"Spare me your maidenly modesty."

He had no idea how apt a description *that* was.

"It's nothing I haven't seen before, and often."

Her ears burned at his casual reference to his love-life.

"I had hoped that we could put this off for a day or two, but I'm needed in Hawaii to close a very important deal," he went on.

"Can we have this conversation when I'm not naked and dripping wet, please?"

Marco clenched his teeth. The images that statement evoked were so erotic he nearly hauled her slippery body out of the tub so he could show her just what he could accomplish while she was naked and dripping wet.

He had thought that by walking in on her bath he could remove the mystery, and in so doing remove some of her allure. But far from it. The hints of peachy skin he could see beneath the water had him hard and wanting her with a ferocity that shocked him.

Her attempts to cover herself had pushed her cleavage higher above the surface of the water, and he was having trouble tearing his eyes away so that he could look at her

face when she talked. He'd seen plenty of naked women—
plenty of beautiful, naked women. Why should this one be
special? She shouldn't be. But she was.

"Fine, I'll wait for you in the living room."

As soon as he left the room, Elaine scrabbled out of the
tub. She wrapped a towel around herself and cautiously
peeked into her room. After she'd verified that a certain
arrogant, pain-in-the-butt hunk wasn't in there she set
about looking for something more substantial than the
towel that was currently the only thing separating her from
total exposure.

Privacy? Ha! They were apparently using different
dictionaries.

She opened the closet for the first time, and almost
choked on her tongue. There wasn't a black or navy blue
suit in sight. The closet was filled with clothes that she was
certain bore designer labels, and every last one of them was
as far removed from her general uniform as possible. This
whole arrangement just got better and better. He was still
playing dress-up with her.

She rifled through the clothes. Cashmeres, silks and
cottons. Reds, golds and blues. The small girlish part of
her that generally lay dormant was delighted by the selection. It was like shopping in her own home.

It's like being bought.

And she wasn't going to accept that. But she wasn't
going out to talk to him in a towel either.

She heard Marco pacing the hardwood floor in the
living room. She fingered a beautiful silk dress that hung
on one of the hangers. It bothered her immensely that she
was thinking about wearing it, thinking about what
Marco's reaction might be to it.

She shoved the dress and the clothes next to it aside

fiercely, banishing the thought of Marco's touch burning her through thin silk.

Everything in the closet was extremely feminine, and extremely flimsy. She selected a dress made of a stretch cotton, by far the sturdiest piece of clothing available, and folded it over her arm as she went to look in the dresser for underwear. It wasn't a big surprise that the same man who'd most likely hidden her sensible wardrobe approved of her lingerie.

Her face heated at the thought of his hands on her lacy bras and panties. It seemed so intimate, so unbearably sensual. She picked a pair of red underwear and a matching lace bra. She let her fingers glide over the material. Had Marco touched them like this? Imagined her wearing them? She clenched her thighs together to try and quell the rapid pulse that was beating at their apex. Her nipples beaded shamelessly against the rough terrycloth of the towel that was still wrapped tightly around her.

Elaine put a fierce stop to her runaway imagination. She put the offending underwear on hurriedly, before slipping the wrap dress on and tying the sash around her waist as tightly as possible. The neckline dipped low, and she was tempted to look for a safety pin to bring the edges of the v-neck together.

"Elaine?" Marco's rich voice floated down the hall and she hurriedly left the room. The prospect of him coming into her bedroom was a bit more than her abnormally alert hormones could bear.

Marco turned when he heard Elaine enter the room. He'd hoped that he would have managed to get his rampaging lust under control by the time his new wife had dressed and come out to meet him. And he might have, had she not appeared in the living room looking like every man's fantasy.

The red wrap dress was held onto her luscious body with a bow, making her look like a present that had been wrapped up just for him. A present he wanted very much to unwrap.

His fingers itched to pull the end of the bow and reveal the pearly skin that lay beneath the dress. He ached to see each gorgeous inch of her delectable body laid bare before his eyes, to touch her silken skin, to taste the hollow beneath her throat.

The seam on his pants bit into his growing erection and he shifted, trying to disguise his reaction to her.

"So, now that I'm decent, you were saying…?" She sat on the couch. Her breasts moved with her, their gentle bounce drawing his attention. If she was wearing a bra it was a flimsy lingerie piece, meant to showcase a woman's breasts rather than conceal anything. He could see the perky outline of her nipples through the thin cotton. Would they be pale and pink like the rest of her? He gritted his teeth. She had to be doing this on purpose. No one could look that provocative by accident.

She was even better than he'd given her credit for. The guise of straitlaced businesswoman had put him at ease, but she was slowly dropping the charade and showing glimpses of the real Elaine. She had acted embarrassed when he'd walked in on her during her bath, but he sincerely doubted that a woman so seductive would be put off by something like that.

She'd done a wonderful job concealing the provocative, sexual part of her nature. Despite her reputation she'd nearly managed to convince him that she was an uptight prude. He could see now what a good little actress she was.

The woman sitting in front of him was a woman who *knew* the effect she had on men. Her cheeks were flushed and her eyes were bright, giving her the look of a woman who had recently indulged in hedonistic passions. There was simply no way she could be unaware of the sheer sex appeal that she exuded.

It might be fun to play her game, to take what she was offering for a while, as long as they were both sharing the same home. It was definitely tempting. He knew she had an agenda, but it was of little concern to him. He would be more than able to enjoy her physically and not get snared in her trap.

Later, when the deal with James Preston was ironed out, he would consider taking her up on the offer to use her delectable body.

He cleared his throat and sat in the chair opposite her. He looked to Elaine as if he was readying for a board meeting. Still, looking as formidable as he did, he was the sexiest man she had ever seen.

"What did you do with my clothes?" she asked, one eyebrow quirked.

"They're still in a box somewhere," he said, waving his hand dismissively.

"You didn't think you should consult me before giving my wardrobe a complete overhaul?"

"It needed one. You can trust me on that."

"I don't relish feeling like you're buying me."

He chuckled. "But that's basically what I've done. I'm paying you with Chapman Electronics to be my wife. And if you're going to be playing the part of Mrs. De Luca you need to look the part. Actors are provided with costumes. If it makes you feel better, then look at it that way."

She opened her mouth as if she was going to offer up one of her tart one-liners, then closed it again as if she'd thought better of it.

"You already know that I've been eyeing one of James

Preston's resort properties in Hawaii, and that he's reluctant to sell to me because of my reputation?"

"Yes, I remember. The Hanalei Bay Resort."

James Preston was a legendary hotelier. His resort property on the island of Kauai was the "it" spot for corporate retreats, celebrity weddings, and romantic getaways for the über-wealthy.

He gave her a wry smile. "That's the one."

"Is he still unsure about you?"

"He's getting there, but he wants to meet with me personally before he agrees to anything."

"Naturally."

He nodded. "And of course I'll need to do a thorough sweep of the property before I make a final decision."

"How long will you be gone?"

"*We* shouldn't be gone for more than a couple weeks."

"We?"

"Yes. We."

"What about my job? You just expect me to pick up and go gallivanting off to paradise and leave them in the lurch?"

"Yes, Elaine, I do. Think of this as an extended job interview. If you do things to my satisfaction, in the end you'll get the company. However, if my goals are compromised so are yours. Remember that."

Marco could see the war that was being waged behind her eyes. The fierce light that had glinted in their blue depths when she'd thought about arguing, the anger when she'd realized she had no choice but to accompany him, to hold to her end of the contract. Then, finally, he'd seen acceptance.

"When do we leave?"

CHAPTER SIX

THE vibrant colour of the island rushed up into Elaine's vision as the plane began to move closer to the viridian land. The trees were so dense she could hardly see the runway, and it felt as though the plane was going to crash into the thick palms and kukuis that lined the coast.

"It's so beautiful," she said.

Marco barely looked up from his laptop. He was sitting across from her in a captain's chair that was adjacent to the small loveseat she was perched on.

His private plane was the size of her apartment, and was lavishly furnished. She'd probably looked completely gauche when she'd boarded the plane back in New York, her mouth hanging open as she took in the absolute indulgence and luxury of her surroundings.

"Yes. It is. Which is why it's such valuable real estate."

Even the matter-of-fact statement sent a shiver of wanting through her. He could recite baseball statistics and still sound unbearably sexy. She'd had her own bedroom and *en suite* bathroom for the duration of the thirteen-hour flight, but not even that little bit of privacy had been enough to keep her from feeling horribly, embarrassingly aware of the man.

It bordered on being infuriating. Where was her focus? She was so close—twelve months away—to reaching the ultimate prize, and half of her mind, and all of her body, were homed in on Marco.

Maybe it was the natural order. Maybe hormones and normal adult desires could only be ignored and suppressed for so long. Maybe they'd spent the last ten years building up in her system, only to be unleashed on the first desirable male to come within five feet of her.

It wasn't as though she'd never had the opportunity. There had been plenty of men who'd showed interest in her, especially in college. And she'd even liked some of them, dated some of them. But in the end their lack of ambition had made her crazy, while her driving need for success had driven them away. There had been kisses— none of them overly passionate, all of them ending at the front door. There had never seemed to be the time or the adequate desire for a physical relationship.

And then there had been Daniel. Whom she'd liked a lot. Whom she'd been attracted to—whom she'd very nearly said yes to when he'd asked that all-important question at the door. But in the end she'd turned down his request to come in, nerves or maybe even morals stopping her from accepting.

That moment of refusal had changed everything. The next day Daniel had started spreading the rumors, and by the end of the day everyone *knew* why she'd been getting promoted. At least they'd thought they did. Nobody would believe that she'd gotten the promotions on her own merit, and her co-workers had been more than willing to believe that she'd slept with the boss rather than believing she might actually be good—better than they were—at what she did. And just like that her career had been killed before it had started.

Which brought her full circle to where she was now. On a private plane that had just landed in Hawaii, with her mercenary husband, whom she was appallingly attracted to, and twelve months of marriage to a man who threw her thoroughly off kilter looming ahead of her.

Marco stood when the plane came to a halt, his laptop secured in its travel case. "We will go straight to the Hanalei Bay Resort and get settled into our accommodations. Later we will be having dinner with James and his wife."

"Our accommodations? As in, we're sharing?"

Marco watched as hectic color flooded Elaine's face. It was a source of amazement to him that a woman of her age could blush so easily. He preferred a more sophisticated type of woman, the kind of woman who didn't expect anything from a man but a few nights of mutual satisfaction. The only sort of pink any of those women got in their cheeks came from their make-up bag. He found it an interesting sort of challenge, making her blush.

"No, actually I was planning to have you installed down the hall, so that I could use your services by day and entertain my mistress by night."

Color reddened her neck and slowly climbed into her face, staining her cheeks a deep crimson. "Well, the stipulations of the prenup would certainly allow it," she said stiffly.

He chuckled. "You're not getting rid of me so easily, *cara mia*." He strode across the cabin of the plane and leaned down, cupping her chin and tilting her face up so that she was forced to meet his eyes. "I'm here to play devoted husband." He smoothed his thumb along her lush bottom lip. Lust attacked him, hot and hard. "And we're on our honeymoon. That means you will be staying very, very close to me."

Her tongue darted out to moisten her lips and the pink tip slicked across his thumb. Electricity shot from his hand to his groin. Her eyes widened, her pupils dilated. She wanted him. She probably wanted his money even more, but there was no denying that she wanted him physically.

And he ached to take her. To pull her to the floor and have his way with her, pound into her while those gorgeous, endless legs were wrapped high around his waist, as she whispered soft, feminine sounds of pleasure in his ear.

He was so hard it hurt.

But he didn't have any protection with him—and not by accident. He wasn't taking any chances with this mercenary woman he'd married. His own parents had given him an early crash course in the essence of human nature. Greed and self-satisfaction were at the core of every human being. Even the most honest and good could be corrupted for the right amount. With enough incentive a father could throw his family out onto the streets to fend for themselves. A mother could leave her children when she got a better offer than sleeping in alleyways. Yes, the right incentive could entice people to commit all kinds of sins.

He didn't trust the woman. Her motives were anything but pure. He was certain of that. She had lied to her own father and married a stranger, all for her personal gain. He had no intention of falling prey to her. She was a fabulous manipulator. She was a calculating businesswoman, the embodiment of sex appeal, a ruthless competitor…and a blushing innocent?

Until he was able to ascertain exactly what her true motives were, exactly which of the characters she portrayed reflected the real woman, he would have to keep his distance.

His erection pulsed in protest.

She turned her face away and picked up her purse. When she faced him again her composure was intact. The face of the flustered girl covered by the mask of a perfectly collected, icy businesswoman.

She was either a very good actress or a very naïve young woman who was in way over her pretty blond head. It bothered him immensely that he wasn't able to figure it out for certain.

She pushed past him, and the tips of her breasts brushed lightly against his chest. Her eyes widened fractionally and she hurried to break the contact. It seemed natural, like an honest mistake. But if there was one thing he knew about women it was that they practiced looking natural until they had it honed to a fine art.

"Well, there had better be two beds." She craned her long, elegant neck and lowered her eyelids, the light lashes fanning across her cheekbones.

He studied her beautiful, haughty profile. Everything about her was designed to entice men. Even, he was discovering, her ice queen routine. She was a challenge—a challenge that roused something in the most primitive, unenlightened, masculine part of him.

A man who really understood female beauty would be able to see hers—be able to appreciate the rarity of it, the quality, even buried beneath the layers of boardroom armor. And any man who recognized her beauty would want a taste of it. Would want to draw from her a response. Would want to make her shed her inhibitions, to take the tight knot of her hair down and sift it through his fingers. Kiss her, make her cry out in pleasure. Make her lose every bit of that hardened exterior until she was soft, pliant, and all out of that control she seemed to prize so much.

He was beginning to think she'd been cleverer in crafting her persona than he could have imagined.

He chuckled at her uptight expression. "I don't think honeymoon suites are typically outfitted with two beds. Unless the newly married couple wants to experience a change of scenery now and then, I don't really see the point."

"If this is some sort of childish trick to get me into bed…"

He reached out and hooked an arm around her slender waist and drew her close to his body. "I don't have to stoop to subterfuge to get a woman to sleep with me." He trailed his finger along the line of her collarbone, and he didn't miss the shiver of awareness that racked her slight frame.

She wiggled, extricating herself from his hold. "Well, I'm not going to become another of the legions of notches on your bedpost. Besides, if you add any more notches the whole bedframe is going to collapse—and where would that leave you and your lovers?"

"The floor."

Elaine's heart stuttered. Images of twined tanned and lily-white limbs flashed through her mind's eye. Marco kissing her passionately, desire overwhelming them to the point that they couldn't make it to the bed, Marco taking her gently to the floor, settling between her thighs…

She blinked, trying to stop the erotic slideshow.

The look in Marco's dark eyes told her that they were experiencing a moment of identical thought, and that was enough to bring common sense and sanity back.

"Classy." She sounded prissy even to her own ears.

"Class is sometimes overrated. Particularly in the bedroom."

The fact that he was always ready with some casual, off-the-cuff response was infuriating. She couldn't hope to compete with him there. She lacked both the sophistication and the experience to fake nonchalance when he said things like that. Before this moment sex on the floor had never even crossed her mind, and she was way too busy grappling with the new, unsettling notion to try and be witty.

"Where is my luggage?" she asked, hoping he wouldn't comment on the abrupt subject change.

His wicked half-smile told her he knew exactly what had prompted her to shift the gears of the conversation. "One of my flight staff will see that it gets put in the rental car."

She held back a comment about the excesses of having staff on a private plane. They were going to be meeting James Preston soon and they were supposed to look like blissed-out newlyweds, not tense strangers.

She followed Marco out of the plane and into the balmy outdoors. A warm salt breeze was blowing in off the sea. The tang from the salt mingled with the smell of moisture and tropical flowers to create a heady perfume. It smelled like sensuality, and it made her acutely conscious of her body. And Marco's.

"Aloha oe."

They stepped onto the tarmac and a woman with glossy black hair and burnished copper skin slipped a fresh flower *lei* over Elaine's head, then Marco's. Elaine didn't think it was her imagination that the double-cheek-kiss the woman planted on Marco lingered longer than was strictly necessary.

"Aloha," Marco said, his husky voice making the word sound exotic and sexy—like an invitation. An invitation to engage in bedpost-demolishing activity. It wasn't as

though she could blame the woman. Marco was a walking advertisement for the pleasures of the flesh.

Elaine saw the woman slip a card into the pocket of Marco's pants and a strange, heated emotion rolled through her stomach, causing it to cramp and twist. Jealousy? She'd never actually experienced the emotion before, and it wasn't the time or the place to start feeling it now. Or the *man* to feel it for.

A glossy silver Mercedes McLaren was parked near the edge of the tarmac, the convertible top down, the keys in the ignition. She ought to have figured that Marco didn't go to the rental counter like mere mortals.

Marco opened the passenger door, his smile aimed only at her. He looked every inch the devoted husband. He wouldn't have any trouble convincing James Preston he'd reformed.

As long as he doesn't convince you.

She brushed the thought aside as soon as it popped into her mind. She didn't care if he did truly reform and decide he wanted love, commitment, and two point four kids. He could find them with some other woman who actually *wanted* those things. She wanted to realize her full potential, not become a casualty of marriage—a mere accessory to a husband who valued her about as much as he did his brand-new Rolex.

She'd seen it happen to her mother. Seen the decline of her self-esteem. Seen her make an absolute fool of herself over male attention, craving validation from her husband and, when that failed, from her many young lovers, unable to find value in herself. Elaine had vowed she would never be that woman. She would never pin her hopes, dreams and sense of self-worth on someone else.

Marco put his hand on the small of her back, and she

all but leapt into the car to escape the burn of his touch through her thin button-up blouse. The cool, butter-soft leather of the seat helped to douse some of the flames that his touch had ignited, but the embers still burned in her veins. She hoped he didn't notice how much he affected her physically. One look at his dazzling grin as he sank into the car told her he was acutely, absolutely aware of what he did to her.

The virgin and the playboy. It was an unfair pairing. She had never felt this level of desire for a man in her life, and she certainly didn't have any practice suppressing it.

The high-performance engine roared to life and Marco tapped the gas pedal, taking the sleek sports car from zero to sixty in a fraction of a second.

Elaine's eyes widened when she looked at the speedometer. "Slow down!"

Marco took a sharp corner on the narrow two-lane road with ease. "A car like this isn't meant for slow."

After a few moments she relaxed. The car handled with total precision, and Marco was in complete control of the roaring beast. He tamed it, harnessed its power, drawing from it the response he wanted—a response only he could command…and just like that her mind was back on sex.

He had that effect on women, *all* women, she thought sourly, as she remembered the forward actions of the gorgeous native woman.

"Did that…did that woman at the airport give you her phone number?"

He reached into his pocket and pulled out the card, setting it in Elaine's lap. "I hadn't checked."

The digits on the card confirmed what Elaine had suspected. "That's nice. We're here on our honeymoon and she's trying to pick you up."

He chuckled, low and throaty. "It makes a case for there being two beds in our honeymoon suite."

Her face heated, but not from embarrassment this time. "That's disgusting."

"You're the one who made the rules of the arrangement, Elaine."

"I hardly imagined you bringing another woman back to our *shared* hotel room."

"Give me a bit more credit than that," he said, sounding darkly amused. "It isn't as though I've slept with every woman I've been photographed with. My bedpost actually remains pretty sturdy."

She didn't know why, but the knot of tension that had settled in her chest loosened a fraction. "I guess we're both victims of false press."

He shrugged. "It's all part of having ambition. There are a lot of people who want to get to the top. They want fame and fortune, and if they have to take others down in the process they're more than willing. Your downfall opened doors for more than one person at your firm, didn't it?" She nodded in the affirmative. "It's probably why your colleagues latched onto it with so much glee. Your descent from grace was the secret to their success."

"I guess I lack the killer instinct. Maybe I should have spread some gossip of my own."

"I sincerely doubt you lack the killer instinct." He reached over and took her left hand, lifting it so that her engagement ring and newly acquired wedding band caught the sunlight. "This is proof."

"What does it say about you, then?" she huffed.

He laughed. "No one has ever accused me of being a soft touch."

Not outside the bedroom. He didn't have to add that last

part, her imagination did it all by itself. She imagined that in bed he could be a soft touch, or a demanding touch—whatever his lover desired.

She slammed the brakes on her runaway imagination and concentrated instead on the lush scenery that surrounded them. The water was clear and brilliant. Spinner dolphins swam alongside the coastline, seeming to follow them as they drove down a road that was slowly winding up the heavily forested green mountainside.

The road dead-ended at the top of the mountain, ending at a heavy wrought iron gate with a number pad and intercom mounted on it. Marco leaned in and entered a series of numbers with his long tanned fingers. She couldn't stop herself from enjoying his hands again.

The gates opened and they continued up the steep drive.

The hotel was built into the side of the mountain, the balconies for each room segmented and private, overlooking an impossibly gorgeous bay with surreally bright water and a luxuriant natural landscape, with an abundance of vibrant tropical blooms.

Everything on the island seemed like a sensory overload to her. The air was thick with salt from the ocean; mist was rising from the fresh rainfall and the perfume of flowers. The colors were overly saturated. The blanket of green that covered the mountain was thick and dense, a shocking contrast to the ever-brownish haze of smog that blanketed the city of New York. It was like having a veil ripped from her eyes and having her five senses fully realized for the first time.

Not necessarily a good thing, since her awareness of the man who was her temporary husband had also gone up several notches.

Marco slipped his arm around her waist and led her to

the front entrance of the hotel. Pink and orange sunset vines clung to the stone exterior. Far from giving it a rustic appearance, the invasion of nature upon the man-made structure made it look all the more exclusive.

A small crew of sharply dressed men exited the hotel and greeted them with broad smiles. A young man with blond hair shook Marco's hand firmly. "*Aloha*, Mr. De Luca. Mr. Preston is in a meeting, and is regretful he is not able to greet you and your new bride. My name is Jonathan, and I would love to take care of any needs you might have. The Ano Lani villa has been reserved for you. It's nearly half a mile up the coastline. If you like, myself or one of the other men can drive you and assist in the unloading of your luggage."

"Thank you, but it won't be necessary. Perhaps just a map of the resort?"

Jonathan reached into his suit jacket and pulled out a sleek brochure. "If there is anything else in particular you need, the concierge will be pleased to see to it."

"I don't think the charger for my BlackBerry made it into my luggage," Marco said. "I would like to have one delivered to the villa as soon as possible."

After receiving the make and model information Jonathan and crew went back into the hotel to complete their mission.

It was amazing the kind of service money could buy. Her family were well off by most standards, but they would hardly have been able to aspire to be guests at a place like this. Marco only had to sign a check and he would *own* it. The intensity of that amount of wealth, that amount of power, was staggering. She understood why he was concerned with guarding his assets. Even the most scrupulous of people would be tempted to try a taste of what Marco enjoyed so freely.

She wondered if he even realized just how incredible it was that he was in such a position. He probably didn't. He had been born into wealth, and from it had fashioned almost immeasurable riches. No wonder he was so arrogant. Asking him to understand her position was like asking Zeus to step down from Mount Olympus to play cards.

"You didn't forget your charger," she said accusingly as she got back into the small sleek car. As if he would forget any detail—no matter how small.

He shrugged. "No. But I will be keeping Jonathan on as an employee if he manages to show up with one in the villa in the next couple of hours."

"Testing the staff?"

"Why not? I'm not an easy boss to please, Elaine. I don't coddle employees. At a resort of this level I will expect nothing less than impeccable service from those who work here. I would like to keep the passing of the hotel's ownership as smooth as possible. Keeping the same staff would help immensely. However, I'm not running a charity here, which means I expect perfection or they don't have jobs."

Marco glanced over at her. Her expression was disapproving. A little line creased her alabaster forehead, and her mouth was pursed into an ungenerous pucker.

"You have a problem with this?" he asked, entertained by her show of humanity.

"It doesn't really seem fair to just fire someone if they don't get a BlackBerry charger to you in time."

"If you're going to run a company you're going to have to adopt the same mindset I have. Time is money—clichéd, but very true. When people on your staff waste time, they waste your money. When they leave a client dissatisfied, they cost you money. You have good ideas, but if you can't execute them, if you can't hire a team to *help* you execute them, you won't get anywhere."

The crease between her brows deepened. "I guess I'm a walking example of the lows one has to stoop to in order to make it in the business world."

He laughed darkly. "Just treat everyone the way you treat me and you'll have no trouble being ruthless."

"There's a thought."

Marco watched as Elaine's expression changed from one of recalcitrance to one of wonder.

The car eased around the last curve and the villa came into view.

The Ano Lani villa was made secluded by dense native foliage, and a pond had been built to encircle the house, with a small wooden bridge granting the only access into the grand structure. Floor-to-ceiling windows exposed the villa to billion-dollar views of the crystalline water and the surrounding mountains. It was obvious that the villa itself, no matter how stunningly luxurious, was only a part of what the guests were paying for. The real star was the serene natural beauty of the bay.

"This is… I suppose people pay a lot of money to stay in a place like this?"

He nodded. "Thousands of dollars a night. And with the proper marketing they would pay more than that."

"I can see why you want it."

"It will be a nice addition. Normally I build my resorts from the ground up, but the Hanalei Bay area is essentially full, and new construction wouldn't be practical."

They got out of the car, and Marco pulled their luggage out of the trunk of the small vehicle.

Elaine followed, the sight of her temptingly long legs

stretching from the McLaren almost more temptation than his starved libido could handle.

"Did you always know you wanted to get into real estate? Your father did manufacturing, didn't he?" she asked.

Coldness invaded his chest—that chill that always pervaded his being when he thought of his bastard of a father. "My father had no bearing whatsoever on my chosen field." His voice was hard, clipped, and he could tell by the wounded doe look in her eyes that it had shocked her. He didn't really care at that moment. "I've built my business from nothing. It was pure accident that I got work at a real estate office, but not accidental at all that I chose to excel at it—and everything else my corporation has ventured into over the past thirteen years."

He'd figured she would pry further. It was inevitable. Women always wanted to know what a man was thinking. Instead she averted her eyes and began a closer inspection of the villa.

She hurried across the little wooden bridge, running a slender, elegant hand over the rail in a movement so unconsciously seductive that all thoughts of his father were driven straight from his mind. The way her delicate fingers caressed the wood was symbolic in ways he did not need to dwell on.

She walked up the stairs and onto the wraparound deck. He didn't even try to keep his eyes from lingering on her curvaceous figure, on her pert little bottom and her narrow waist.

He noticed that her shoulders visibly sagged with relief when she walked into the expansive living room. "Plenty of places to sleep," she said softly.

He should have had them remove everything but the bed, so that she was forced to choose between the bamboo floor or a night in his arms. Although he'd told her the honest truth when he'd said he'd never had to coerce a woman into his bed. Women usually went all too willingly. But something about her resistance was enticing in a way he hadn't imagined it could be. Of course, something different and new when it came to sex was a rarity for a man of his experience. It was no wonder he found her so intriguing.

He was used to blatant women. Women who stared openly with hungry eyes and practically begged him to take them before they even made it to dinner on the first date. He was a man who enjoyed sex, and had a healthy appetite for it, but lately the game had started to turn him off. It had all started to seem vaguely distasteful. Which was why he'd put off finding an available woman to take the edge off his desire. And probably why Elaine looked as tempting as original sin.

"We'd better get ready for dinner."

Elaine jumped when Marco's husky voice penetrated her thoughts. She turned to look at him and her heart did that weird flipping thing it did whenever she was caught off-guard by his sheer masculine beauty. Which was every time she looked at him.

She might need to get ready for dinner, but he looked as perfect as ever. Not a dark, gleaming hair out of place, his white shirt unbuttoned at the collar, the sleeves pushed up, revealing those delicious forearms again. His black trousers didn't have a wrinkle. With her blond hair frizzing from the humidity, and her blouse and pants showing every hour of the long journey, she felt like one big crease standing next to his perfectly pressed beauty.

She gratefully escaped to the luxurious bathroom. Standing there with him, in a space that was made for lovers, had probably housed hundreds of them, had seemed much too intimate. And, if she was honest, too tempting. She suddenly knew why it had been so hard for all the girls in high school and college—why so many of them had made fools of themselves over boys. It had been easy for her to act above it all, but the simple fact was that she'd never desired a man in a sexual way before—not truly. Now that she did, she understood the struggle.

There was something about attraction that she'd missed before. She'd liked men, had felt little bouts of butterflies in her belly when the object of her affection had walked by. But this…this was different. There was something primitive about it. A physical response that was unrelated to any of the finer feelings she possessed. She might not have any experience with sex, but her body knew what it wanted. And its demands were getting louder with each passing minute spent in her *husband's* company.

She pulled her make-up case out of her luggage and set it on the marble countertop. She turned the handle on the basin sink and splashed cold water on her face and her pulse points in an effort to cool her heated hormones down to a low simmer.

There was no curtain for the shower, only a thick, clear panel of glass. So no privacy—although she had a feeling that she'd have to shower in a sweater and pants to feel comfortable with Marco so near. Especially given what had happened the last time she'd gotten naked with him nearby. The memory of him walking in on her in the tub made her feel hot with embarrassment. At least that was what she was pretending the heat was from.

She stripped quickly and stepped into the shower, not minding that the water was cool. She rinsed as quickly as possible and ran a razor over all the necessary places before hopping out and dressing in the simple, figure-hugging coral cocktail dress that had been pre-selected by Marco for the all-important dinner.

In a rare moment of honesty she admitted to herself that it wasn't the prospect of being walked in on by Marco that had made her cut her shower short. The pulsing spray of the water on her sensitized skin had been too much for her already fired-up hormones to handle. It had made her think of his hands, his fingertips, gliding over her body, and the heavy ache of her breasts and the dull pulsing between her thighs had reached a nearly unbearable level.

She finished getting ready as quickly as possible, tying her frizzing hair into a loose bun and applying a thin layer of make-up before putting on the ridiculous high heels that Marco had chosen for her to pair with the dress. She hurried back into the living room, still fastening the clasp on her delicate silver necklace.

"Ready?" Marco looked as though he'd also just stepped out of the shower, his dark hair damp and curling at the nape of his neck.

She closed her hands into fists, letting the bite of her nails on the tender skin of her palms ground her in reality as she fought the urge to cross the room and sift her fingers through his damp curls. Her heartbeat quickened its pace and a surge of longing washed over her.

She licked her suddenly dry lips. "Yes." Her shaking fingers slipped and she missed the clasp on the necklace.

"Need any help?"

Her heart pounded harder. She was sure, absolutely sure, that he could hear it. "Yes… No…"

He chuckled. "You aren't sure if you need help?"

I'm certain I do need help.

But not the kind he meant. If she were even the tiniest

bit sane she would have refused his offer. But it had been one temptation too many.

He moved behind her, his warm, moist breath fanning across her neck. She felt an answering wetness building between her thighs. He put his hand on her nape, his fingers lightly massaging her in small circles, and pleasure radiated from his touch and spread through her body. Her knees started to feel unsteady.

"You'll have to let go, Elaine."

Oh, she was. She was letting go of everything. Of everything she'd ever believed to be true about herself—of every conviction, every tightly held belief. There was no room for anything but this moment, and everything else—all the fear and the doubt—had to go unheeded.

"Elaine, let go of the necklace."

Her fingers released their hold on the dainty silver chain and a hot flush stole across her cheeks.

His skillful fingers moved against the sensitive skin, and far too soon he'd finished fastening the clasp for her. He pulled his hands away, and the loss of his touch left her feeling bereft somehow.

Slowly the fog of her arousal, the fog that had descended the moment they'd entered this tropical paradise, began to lift. She couldn't let this happen. He was the kind of man who used and discarded women with all the ease that most people had changing socks—definitely not the kind of man to get involved with. Even if he hadn't been the absolute wrong man, it was absolutely the wrong time for her to get involved with someone. But that didn't stop the restless ache of desire that left her feeling hollow and unsatisfied.

"Thank you," she murmured, hoping he didn't notice the throaty tone her voice had suddenly adopted. She stepped away from him, hoping that distance would bring some sort of relief from the intense, unconscionable attraction that she felt for him.

He reached out and took her hand, drawing her back into the warmth of his body. "Ready for dinner, *amore mia*?"

CHAPTER SEVEN

MARCO couldn't help but be impressed with Elaine's performance over dinner. She came across as bright, confident and witty. James Preston was eating from the palm of her hand in a matter of minutes. The older man was completely taken in by her charm and intelligence. Which Marco knew should please him. Instead, primal possessiveness surged through him.

He moved closer to Elaine, wrapping his arm around her delicate waist and drawing her to him, smoothing his fingers along her silk-covered flesh. He felt a slight tremor race through her body at the light contact.

"So, Marco," James said, sliding nearer to his own wife, "I understand you find it old-fashioned of me to have a vested interest in what will become of the resort when I retire and sell out. But I built it up from the ground. This was my first great success and it has sentimental meaning to me. I want to be sure that I'm passing it on to someone who will preserve the integrity of the property."

"And I intend to. I will be keeping it privately owned, so that I retain total control of what goes on. My vision is to keep it exclusive—perhaps even make it more so." Marco began to outline his plan for creating an even more exclusive clientele base for the hotel, while increasing profits and improving the local economy.

"And your lovely wife will be involved in the process?" James gave Elaine a glowing look, and Marco tightened his hold on her.

"*My* wife will be as involved as she wishes." He couldn't keep the biting edge from his voice.

James raised his gray eyebrows. "Well, he's quite possessive, isn't he?" He directed his question to Elaine.

A mischievous glint shone in her eyes. "Marco's such a charming antique." She ran a slender hand down his arm and gave him a look that was so falsely adoring he could have laughed had he not been so concerned about the words that were coming out of her mouth. "He has quite a reputation with women, as I'm sure you know, but I've tamed him pretty successfully. Of course there are moments when his inner caveman appears."

James's redheaded wife Kim quirked a smile, and spoke for the first time since they'd sat down at the dinner table. "Isn't that the way it is with all men?"

"You behave," James said playfully.

And just like that the tone of the conversation swayed from business and onto personal topics.

Marco had to admit that Elaine had a way with people. She could be engaging when she wanted to be, and none of her usual frosty reserve was on display for the Prestons.

Marco made an appointment to meet with James in the morning, and cut the dinner short before more drinks. As a rule he didn't drink much. He didn't like to dull his senses. And around Elaine Chapman he was going to need his mind functioning at its best. The last thing he needed was to have his decisions made through the soft, smoky haze of alcohol.

She walked ahead of him out of the restaurant, her hips swaying, encased lovingly in that form-fitting little dress. She was like a bright tropical flower, or a piece of luscious fruit. Forbidden fruit. He had made her off-limits. A notion that was completely foreign to him. A notion that made her appear all the more succulent.

She moved to the passenger side of the car, her body hidden from him by the dark shadows of the azalea bushes that lined the asphalt. He caught up to her and pulled her against him. The little hitch in her breath was the only sound she made to express her surprise. "So I'm a caveman, am I?" He placed his hands on her waist and drew her nearer, allowing her to feel the steel of his erection pressed against the curve of her bottom.

"It's not the first time I've said it," she said, her voice breathless.

"You were supposed to behave yourself," he growled low, bringing his lips so close to her ear that he brushed the tender skin.

"You mean I was supposed to play silent accessory, like James's wife?"

"Men like women who do as they're told." He skimmed his fingers from the indent in her waist to the underside of her breasts.

"Well, that's too bad. I don't suppose I'll be having much luck with men."

He chuckled. "*Cara mia*, I don't believe that for a moment. You are walking temptation."

She drew in a breath. "Even when I'm being mouthy?"

"Especially then."

She leaned her head back for a moment, her body relaxing, her curves molding to fit against him. He pressed a kiss to her neck and she stiffened. "Stop."

He released her. "Why?" Somewhere between the restaurant and the car he'd decided he didn't need to fight his
attraction for her anymore. As long as he stayed in control
of the situation, and there was no doubt that he would,
there could be no harm in indulging in an affair with her.
He found it easy to indulge in the pleasures of the flesh
without engaging his emotions, and in his experience a
modern woman viewed sex much the same way.

Elaine lowered her eyes. "It will make things…compli-
cated."

He cupped her cheek and tilted her face up, forcing her
to meet his gaze. "There's nothing complicated about sex."

"Maybe not for you."

But Elaine knew that for her it would be. Dinner had
been akin to torture. Watching him talk business, seeing
him in his element, a ruthless light in his eyes as he spoke
about his plans for the resort, the confidence he exuded,
the arrogance… It had been the most spectacularly sexy
thing she'd ever seen in her life. More than that, he'd made
her *feel* far too much. Not just desire, but other things.
She'd been proud of him, had felt possessive. She hadn't
liked the way Kim Preston had eyed Marco's spectacular
physique—not that she could blame the other woman—
but then Elaine's gaze had locked on the platinum wedding
band on Marco's left hand and one word had run through
her mind: *mine*.

And that was wrong. He wasn't hers. And he never
could be. Neither should she want him to be!

She felt as if she was dangling from the last thin shred
of her resistance. If she let go, if she lost her grip, she was
going to go tumbling down into the abyss beneath her, and
climbing back out would be nearly impossible.

"There's nothing complex about this," he said, his voice

a low, sexy whisper that vibrated through her, sending shockwaves of longing through her being. "This is the most basic thing in the world. Man and woman. Desire and satisfaction."

The promise in his voice almost stole her resolve then and there. "Marco, I'm tired and jet lagged. Let's go back to the villa."

She knew the absence of a firm no coming from her lips did not escape his notice. She honestly hadn't been able to muster up the will to give him one. She knew it was dangerous, going back to the Ano Lani without a definitive decision in place, but maybe that was what she wanted. She was honest enough to admit, at least in that moment, that she wanted to leave the door open a little bit. She didn't want to lose all possibility of making love with him—not when so much of her desired it so intensely.

They took the ride back to the hotel in silence. Elaine tried to steady her breathing, to get a handle on the riot of sensations and emotions that were tumbling through her usually predictable body. Where was her cool head now? When she most needed that level, analytical part of her personality it had deserted her like a rat off a sinking ship. Almost as if it wanted no part in the impending disaster.

No. There would be no disaster. She could control herself. The problem was that she wasn't entirely certain she *wanted* to control herself.

She leapt from the car the moment it came to a stop in front of the villa, needing desperately to put some distance between Marco and herself so that she could clear her head.

She felt rather than heard him enter the room behind her. "I'll sleep on the couch," she offered quickly. "You're a lot…bigger than I am."

He shrugged. "Suit yourself. I have some work to finish up before I head to bed. I'll be in the office."

"Did the BlackBerry charger show up?"

He chuckled, the sound spreading through her like melting butter. "As a matter of fact it did."

"So the staff shall live to see another day?" She didn't know why she was instigating conversation, why she was so reluctant to let him go, to let him end the evening. She hadn't completely closed the door on them making love tonight, but he obviously had. She should be relieved.

"So long as their performance remains up to par."

He turned away from her, and she couldn't keep herself from admiring the view. The broad set of his shoulders, his lean waist and his muscular butt were far too tempting a treat to pass up. She had to get her thrills somewhere. And before Marco it had been a long time since she'd gotten any. And those had been innocent thrills, mild in comparison to the kind of sensations that were pinging through her body now, electrifying the blood that was charging through her veins.

"I'll probably just go to bed," she said.

Marco turned and watched her look forlornly at the long couch. She was probably weighing her need to keep up her hard-to-get act versus her need for a good night's sleep—although she wouldn't find a good night's sleep on the couch *or* in his bed.

He went into the office without bothering to watch her make her final decision. His body ached with need and it unsettled him. Yes, it had been a long time since he'd been with a woman, much longer than he was accustomed to, but that did not excuse the intensity of the desire that had him hard, throbbing, and unable to concentrate.

Ironic that he had never come close to proposing

marriage to a woman in his life, and the one he *had* married seemed to avoid physical contact with him at all costs. But she desired it as he did. She wanted him too. But something was stopping her from making the final step. It could all be part of her act—playing at reluctance in order to build his level of sexual frustration to a fever pitch. Or she could be genuinely opposed to conducting a physical relationship. He couldn't discount that possibility.

But, whatever her reasoning, he was still left with a raging hard-on and no satisfaction in sight.

He clenched his fists and turned his attention to his laptop, trying to turn his normally high-performing mind to the task at hand. It was a futile attempt. His body was talking much louder than his brain tonight.

And he wasn't the type of man to practice self-denial.

Despite the fact that as far as her body was concerned it was the early hours of the morning, she knew she was far too keyed-up to get any sleep. She wandered through the villa, pausing to enjoy the native Hawaiian-style artwork before wandering into the bathroom.

She needed a bath to settle her mind and her body. But the bathroom that was at the "safe" end of the villa—the end that didn't take her anywhere near Marco's office or bedroom—only had a shower, and she was desperate for her nightly ritual.

She opened the glass door that led to the outdoor courtyard. Low stone walls and a vine covered lattice roof offered privacy, but also allowed her to see the jade-green bay, turned gray by the silver moonlight.

A massive jet tub sat in the corner of the courtyard. A freestanding wooden rack with towels and a white silk bathrobe was situated by the tub. She sighed. Stress relief was at hand. It wouldn't relieve any of her other physical issues, but it would help loosen her knotted shoulders.

She turned the gilded taps and experimented with the assorted essential oils that had been placed on the towel rack. Candles were placed on the four corners of the tub, and a lighter had been left nearby. She bent over and lit each candle. It was the perfect setting. Relaxing. Sensual. Romantic. It was a bath designed for two. But only one would be taking it. And it was better that way.

She slipped out of her clothes quickly, her eyes darting to the door, praying that Marco didn't pick that moment to explore this portion of the villa, and stepped into the tub. Or maybe, a treacherous voice spoke up, it would be more interesting if he did. She banished the unapproved thought and sank beneath the water, letting the scent of mint and vanilla wash over her, relaxing her body and her mind.

It was so easy to imagine Marco sitting behind her, her head pillowed on his muscular chest, her body wedged between his masculine thighs, the rough hair abrading her soft skin… Her heart began to pound heavily, and her body began to feel a whole different kind of languor.

She stood from the tub abruptly and reached for one of the jade-green towels, drying her over-sensitive skin quickly before wrapping herself in a robe. She stepped out of the water and welcomed the slight bite of the night air. She needed something to cool her down.

She padded over to the far end of the courtyard and out the gate that led to the large wooden deck that was attached to the villa. She leaned against the railing and gazed down into the koi pond, watching the fat orange fish swim lazily through the water. Her heart was still pounding and her breath was coming out in short, uneven bursts.

She drew a shaky hand over her face. She had a

feeling she was fighting a losing battle. Maybe the key was to stop fighting. She wanted Marco. She didn't want to get married for real, and fall in love—at least not in the foreseeable future—but she honestly didn't want to die a virgin either. Not that she'd ever worried about it much before.

If she slept with Marco she ran the risk of getting in too deep. She knew that women sometimes underestimated the effect sex had on them. But if she went into it with her eyes open and viewed it as a learning experience, was able to be detached…maybe then it would work.

"I was looking for you." Marco's husky whisper drew her from her reverie. She turned to face him and her throat dried. He was so impossibly handsome, so amazingly, sensationally masculine. He made everything feminine inside of her quiver with expectant longing.

"I took a bath," she said, hoping the silver moonlight disguised the blush she knew was staining her cheekbones. "It helps me relax."

He moved closer to her, his eyes black in the dim light, the planes of his face thrown into sharp relief. He reached a hand out and cupped her cheek, stroking it lightly with his thumb. She shivered, and she felt her nipples tighten and press against the thin, insubstantial fabric of the robe, her aching flesh calling for his attention, his touch.

He tipped her chin up and she met his eyes, shocked by the stark hunger she saw in them—a hunger that reflected her own. "If I kiss you I won't stop," he said, his voice a rough whisper. "Not until you're naked beneath me, crying out my name."

She licked her lips. He remained still, his uncompromising gaze locked on hers. He was putting her in control, making her take the final step. She couldn't refuse him.

Not again. She didn't have the willpower or the desire to walk away from him.

"Marco." She hoped he didn't notice the tremor in her voice. "Kiss me. Now."

And then his mouth was on hers, hot, hungry and consuming. He pulled her into his body, pressing his insistent arousal against her center. She moved her hips reflexively, and gasped at the sensations that radiated through her.

He parted her lips and thrust his tongue deep into the recesses of her mouth. She let her tongue glide against his, the friction nearly buckling her knees. She had never been kissed like this, so deeply and passionately. The ember that had been smoldering low in her belly caught fire and burned through her, white heat streaking through her veins. Every nerve ending, every cell, was on high alert. Every feeling was magnified. Desire had become something wild and uncontrollable. Want had become need, desperate and as necessary as her next breath.

Marco moved his hand to her waist and the flimsy robe slipped from her body, leaving her totally exposed to the cool night air and to him. He drew back for a moment, taking in the sight of her body. She wanted to cover herself, but fought the urge. She'd never been naked in front of a man before, and she was overwhelmed by a surge of self-consciousness, but she didn't want to look like the gauche virgin that she was. She wasn't about to confess to that. Not now. Not with him. He would probably laugh at her, if he believed her at all. She closed her hands into fists and managed to keep them at her sides.

"You are such a beautiful woman." He stroked her aching nipple with one callus-roughened thumb and she gasped at the exquisite sensation that arrowed from her breast to her core.

A broken cry escaped her lips, and any thoughts of modesty flew from her mind. She moved to embrace him again, pressing her naked body against him, not caring that he was still fully clothed. He gripped her rear end and drew her tightly into him. The buttons of his shirt teased her breasts, his belt buckle, and beneath that his cloth-covered erection, pressed into her belly. This time her knees did give way. Only his firm grasp kept her from melting into a puddle at his feet.

He locked his lips over hers again and smoothed his hands up her body, skimming them lightly over her curves. She was beginning to feel lightheaded. Tension was coiling in her pelvis, so tight it was nearly unbearable. He cupped her breasts with his hands, rolling his thumbs over their taut peaks. The muscles at her feminine core pulsed and she gasped into his mouth.

He removed one of his hands and cursed. He drew away from her and she saw that he'd been reaching for his wallet.

"What?" she asked. Her body was so tense, so needy. She needed his hands again, his mouth.

"I don't have a condom," he said simply.

She laughed weakly, not quite able to believe she was having this conversation with him. "The hotel has an excellent concierge."

He groaned. "It will take far too long. I need you now, *cara mia*."

A thrill of feminine power shot through her. His need was the same as hers. He felt just as desperate and aching and close to the edge.

"I'm on the pill," she blurted, silently thanking the doctor who had suggested she start taking birth control to regulate her cycle.

He looked at her for a moment, his expression implacable. "I'm healthy. I always use condoms. Even when the woman is on some other form of birth control."

"I'm healthy," she promised. On that point she was certain.

And then she was back in his arms, his kisses fierce and possessive. She began to undo the buttons on his crisp white dress shirt with shaking fingers, her heart thundering in her ears. When the shirt fluttered to the floor all she could do was stare dumbly in admiration at the perfection that she had uncovered.

"I want to touch you," she said.

He chuckled. "Be my guest."

His breath came out in a hiss when her cool hands came into contact with his hot, sweat-slicked skin. She could feel his heart pounding heavily beneath her palm, the erratic rhythm mirroring her own. She let her hands roam over his lightly hair-roughened pectoral muscles and down his washboard flat abs, reveling in the hardness and heat that radiated from his gorgeous body. She trailed a finger down the line of hair that disappeared beneath the waistband of his pants.

He sucked in a breath and gripped her wrist, halting her exploration. "I think it's time to find a bed," he ground out.

"I thought you were accustomed to making do with the floor." She didn't recognize the husky, sultry voice that came out of her mouth.

"Minx." He lifted her off her feet and into his arms, taking long strides into the house.

"Caveman," she said, breathless.

He crossed the large villa quickly, his heavy footfalls echoing the pounding of her heart.

"You bring that out in me," he said, setting her on her feet in front of the canopied bed.

"I do?" she asked, her voice breaking as he pressed a kiss to the hollow of her throat.

"Yes. You make me feel dangerously uncivilized."

He kissed the valley between her breasts, and she couldn't have responded to his comment if she'd wanted to. Then he moved his head and took one straining peak into his mouth. She closed her eyes, stars dancing across her vision. Molten desire pooled hot in her belly and dampened her core.

Marco took her hands and placed them on his belt. With shaking fingers she undid the buckle and let it hang loosely. She looked at the outline of his bulging erection, pushing aggressively against his black pants and quickly undid the closure before nerves could overtake her arousal. She lowered the zipper and the back of her hand made contact with his hardened shaft. His body jerked, and he groaned in obvious pleasure.

Emboldened by his response, she encircled his heavy length through the thin fabric and squeezed gently. He closed his eyes and tilted his head back. "You're a dangerous woman."

She laughed shakily and started to work his pants down over his lean hips, taking his underwear with them. It suddenly seemed very important to see him, to get her first glimpse of a naked man, so she could assess exactly what she was dealing with.

The sight of his nude body took her breath away. He was beautiful. He was also very big—much bigger than she'd anticipated a man could be—and she had to wage a small battle with her nerves. She inhaled and wrapped her fingers around him. His skin was even hotter there, like a flame. She moved her hand over his velvety skin, exploring him, learning what he liked and what made him moan with pleasure.

"Enough teasing." He picked her up again and she

found herself lying flat on her back on the cool white comforter.

He drew a nipple into his mouth, sucking it, laving it with the flat of his tongue, before moving his attention to the other breast and repeating the act. Heat flared in her pelvis and all nervousness fled, pushed out by the intense longing that was pouring through her body in waves.

Marco pulled back and looked at her, his eyes glittering with passion. He let a finger drift up her inner thigh, coming close to her pulsing wet center. She shivered, anticipation of the unknown coupled with her intense arousal making the muscles in her legs quiver.

Testing her readiness, he slid the tip of one finger inside of her tight channel. She gasped, her hips bowing up off the bed. "Beautiful," he murmured.

He leaned down, spreading her thighs wide with his broad shoulders. Then he touched the sensitive bundle of nerves with his soft lips.

"Marco!" she pushed against him.

He chuckled and pulled her hands down, pinning them to the bed. He lowered his mouth again, sliding his tongue gently through her damp folds, sucking her moist clitoris. The tension in her pelvis tightened until she thought she would shatter into a million pieces if something didn't give.

He repeated the motion, penetrating her with his tongue, and the tension snapped. Pleasure rolled over her like a tidal wave, and for a moment there was nothing. Nothing but feelings so acute, so all consuming, that they overtook her completely, leaving her spent and breathless in the aftermath.

When she came back to herself Marco was above her, positioning himself at her slick entrance. Her orgasm had taken the edge off her need, but she was still unsatisfied.

She ached for him, for his possession. She cupped his tight buttocks with her hands and urged him forward.

He surged into her—and the pain blinded her for a moment, the tearing sting bringing tears to her eyes. She bit her lip to keep the scream that was building in her throat from escaping and lay rigid beneath him, trying to catch her breath.

"What the—?" He began to move away from her, but she gripped his hips, pulling him back to her.

"No. It's getting better. Just be still for a moment." She wrapped her feet around his calves, anchoring him to her.

Gradually the stinging subsided and gave way to a feeling of fullness that was exquisite beyond words. Arousal flared to life inside her again, all discomfort forgotten.

Marco remained still, the cords of his neck standing out, showing the effort it took for him to maintain self-control.

"Now," she begged.

Then he began to move. The sensation was so shattering, so amazing. She was lost in the steady rhythm of his thrusting. The fractured sounds of their breathing. She felt the muscles in her pelvis spasming. The feeling tightened more still, radiating down to her internal muscles. She was reaching for something—something that seemed much too high for her to grasp.

Then she found it. It was so deep, so all-consuming that she couldn't keep it all inside of her. She let out a hoarse cry as the pleasure rushed up and crashed over her like a wave. She gripped his shoulders, using him as an anchor, as her release went on and on, until finally she was left spent and breathless, floating in the swirling surf.

Marco stiffened above her and pushed himself firmly against her, freezing for a moment while he gave himself up to his own orgasm. He collapsed on top of her and held her close, his accelerated heartbeat reverberating through her, matching the beat of her own.

She brushed a lock of hair out of his eye and traced the features of his face lightly with her fingers. He had shown her a side of herself she hadn't believed existed; he had made her more than she had been.

It was impossible in that moment to shut off the emotion that washed through her. Her heart was full and she felt tears begin to slide down her cheeks. She didn't want to guess at why she felt whole with Marco joined to her... why she felt she might break when he withdrew.

In that moment she was very much afraid that she *was* the naïve fool she'd promised herself she would never become.

CHAPTER EIGHT

MARCO rolled onto his back, his breathing labored, his blood roaring in his ears. His whole body was still on fire from what had been simply the most amazing sexual experience of his life. And the most reckless, stupid act he'd ever committed.

He'd had sex with her without a condom, taking her word for it that she was on birth control. She'd been a virgin. A *virgin*.

He'd never so much as kissed an innocent, and now he'd taken one to bed and initiated her none too gently. He was torn between immense guilt at the realization that he'd taken her virginity, and a building rage at the thought that she might have contrived to trap him.

He turned and looked at the woman lying in bed with him. Tears were rolling down her pink cheeks, her bottom lip, swollen and red from his violent kisses, was trembling. His gut twisted, and guilt overrode the anger.

"Did I hurt you?" he asked, catching a tear with his thumb.

She shook her head and then grimaced. "Well, it didn't hurt for too long."

"Why didn't you tell me that you were a virgin?"

She grimaced at the word. "I didn't think it would matter. I kind of hoped you wouldn't notice, actually. And anyway, you wouldn't have believed me."

"You don't know that." He knew she was right. He would never have believed her. He would have thought it a ploy of some kind—just another tactic to get him to drop his guard and do something stupid and irresponsible. Of course even without her admission he'd managed to be stupid and irresponsible.

A few more tears slid down her cheeks.

"I *did* hurt you," he said.

"No." She swiped at the moisture on her face. "I don't know why I'm crying. I really don't. I'm not normally a crier."

"A woman's first time is very emotional."

Her face pinked. "Are you very experienced in the matter?"

"I can only claim this single experience."

Something that looked like relief flashed in her tearful blue eyes. He'd meant to ask her about her birth control pills, about whether or not they really existed, but he couldn't bring himself to interrogate this new incarnation of Elaine, this vulnerable innocent with the wide, unguarded eyes.

She flushed scarlet and began to search the room visually, carefully avoiding his gaze.

He cupped her chin and turned her face to him gently. "Something you need?"

She blushed to the roots of her blond hair. "I don't have any clothes in here."

He chuckled. "I've seen and tasted every inch of you, *cara mia*. Your modesty is too little, too late."

"Well, that was different. We were…and now we're…"

She pulled hard on the sheets and coiled them around her curvy body, before sliding out from beneath the white duvet and standing up.

"Where are you going?"

Her flush intensified. The spot on her chest where his beard had abraded her delicate fair skin turned a deep mottled rose. "I was going to go get my birth control pills, and then I was going to go to sleep on the couch."

That answered his question about the pills. "You're not sleeping in another room."

"I didn't think that men liked to talk…you know… after…"

"Come back to bed, Elaine. After you get your pills, of course."

She scurried off, her steps restricted by the tightly wrapped sheet.

The woman made absolutely no sense to him. She didn't come across as being naïve or sheltered in any way, and she was extraordinarily beautiful. That she had come to his bed without experience just added another piece to her personal puzzle. He prided himself on being able to read people. Business was about more than numbers: it was about gut feeling, it was about intuition. With Elaine his intuition seemed to be on vacation. He was no closer to figuring her out, or her motives, than when she'd first walked into his office with her outrageous proposal.

She came back into the room, her face pink and fresh-scrubbed, her luscious body wrapped in the silk robe they'd discarded on the porch, the sheet draped over her arm.

"See—I wasn't lying." She waved a small pill packet. "I wouldn't risk the company like that." She placed the pills on the nightstand and stood with her arms wrapped around herself. She looked so young and innocent. Some long-ignored protective instinct had him rising from his position and reaching out to her, drawing her down onto the bed.

"So why did you suddenly decide to go to bed with me? Obviously you've made it a point to save yourself."

She shrugged. "Not really. It's like you said—desire and satisfaction. It's not very complicated." A shuddering breath shook her small shoulders. "I've never really wanted to be with anyone like that, and I didn't see the point of taking the step if it wasn't something I really wanted to do." She hesitated for a moment, and then turned onto her side so that she was facing him. "There was one guy that I thought I might… Well, anyway, when I told him I wasn't ready he seemed okay with it. Then the next day at work I found out he was telling everyone I was off-limits to all the guys in the office because I was the boss's plaything." She gave him a pointed look. "I know you've heard the story. Anyway, I haven't been that inspired to try my hand at relationships again."

Her words held a ring of truth to them, and they sent a sharp pain through his chest. The image of a young, naïve Elaine being dragged through the mud by world-weary cynics, her heart broken, her reputation left in tatters, affected him far more than he was prepared for. He didn't want to be a part of that—part of the ugly world that had stolen her innocence in so many ways. But he *was* a part of it. They had stolen her idealism, her emotional inno-cence, and he had taken that last piece—her physical in-nocence—for himself. He wouldn't use it against her, but he had nothing to offer her either.

"This isn't going to be a relationship in any sort of per-manent sense. That's not how I do things." He despised the bluntness of his words, but he would not give her time to entertain fantasies of a future for the two of them. That was one reason he'd so carefully avoided women with no experience. They thought of love and sex as two things inextricably linked, and he honestly didn't have any of that kind of love available.

She straightened her spine, her blue eyes emotionless. "I know that. And I don't really want a relationship either."

Once again the woman managed to surprise him. She never said or did what he expected her to do. He'd expected her to be clinging to him and asking him about his feelings, but instead she'd been cool, almost aloof, since returning to the bedroom.

"Then what is it you want?"

Her face turned a deep crimson. Now he knew that the blushing wasn't an act. She'd blushed like a virgin because that was exactly what she had been.

"The company," she said, her chin set stubbornly.

"I meant what is it you want from me?" A slow smile curved his lips. "What are your terms and conditions?"

Elaine didn't know how to have a conversation with a naked man. It was difficult to concentrate on words when they were so close, with him naked and her clad only in the thin, barely there robe. All she wanted to do was lean in and kiss his lips, run her hands over his bare skin, feel him filling her again, bringing her the ultimate release. Harder still to tell him what she wanted when she had no idea *what* it was that she wanted or expected.

Could she honestly have a no-strings physical relationship with him?

Yes! her body screamed enthusiastically.

Yes. Her mind confirmed it. When things went back to normal, when Marco was out of her life and she had assumed her position as owner and CEO of Chapman Electronics, her life would be even more consumed by work than it already was. She would never find the time for a relationship. She had to take this, now, while she had the chance.

And when it was over she would always have the sweetest memories of what it was to be held in Marco's arms. She honestly couldn't imagine ever being with another man, sharing the intimacies that she had shared with Marco. Perhaps it was her inexperience, but she really felt repulsed by the idea of another man touching her. That was why she had to seize the moment. Men did it all the time—satisfied physical needs with no feelings involved. Why shouldn't she do it for herself?

"Twelve months. The physical relationship lasts for the duration of the marriage. Neither of us will be unfaithful, and at the end both parties go away with what we agreed upon," she said, shocked by the steadiness of her voice.

He gave her a wicked grin that made her breasts heavy and caused a pulse to start pounding at the apex of her thighs. "A business deal, Ms. Chapman?"

"Is there any other kind, Mr. De Luca?" Far from being steady, her voice was now quivering again, this time at the lascivious intent that was written all over Marco's face.

He wrapped an arm around her waist and pulled the sheet away, revealing her body to him. "I think it's safe to say we're officially mixing business with pleasure." He rubbed the pad of his thumb over one aching nipple and she felt herself melting into him, ready and willing for whatever he wanted to do to her.

His lips closed over hers and conscious thought became difficult. Her heart was thudding heavily, and new, strange emotions were swelling in her chest. She felt her eyes growing wet with tears again. If she could keep this purely physical, if she could stop herself from feeling, then everything would be all right. She could indulge in her craving for Marco and come away unchanged.

The thought of leaving him sent a ripple of pain through her body that matched the pleasure being delivered by his skilled hands. And then all thought became impossible as she was pulled down into the swirling undertow of sensation.

"Good morning." The sound of a husky male voice pulled Elaine from her comatose sleep. Gradually her senses returned to her. There was a large masculine hand splayed across her belly, and she could feel…oh…she could feel Marco's erection pressed against her backside.

The events from the night before came flooding back to her with brutal clarity. She'd slept with Marco. He knew she'd been a twenty-four-year-old virgin. She had agreed to a twelve-month sex only relationship.

She had officially lost her mind.

His hand drifted up and began toying gently with her nipples. She moaned. Yes. She'd lost her mind. And if he kept touching her like that it was going to be lost to her forever.

"Good morning." She tried to squirm out of his hold, away from him and back into a realm where critical thinking was possible, but that only brought her into more forceful contact with his burgeoning hardness. The twitch of his member and the accompanying moan of pleasure sent a shockwave of longing all the way down to her core. She wasn't going to find her sanity anytime soon.

"No need for you to get up. Breakfast will be delivered in a few minutes."

She increased her struggle to get free. "I'm not getting caught naked in your bed!"

"We're newlyweds," he said innocently. "Where else would they expect to find you?"

He rolled over and pinned her on her back, his smile playful. He raised her hands above her head and held them, effectively trapping her. It should have made her angry. It really shouldn't have turned her on. He brought his mouth down and kissed her deeply, passionately. He pushed one hair-roughened thigh between hers and she voluntarily let her legs fall open.

The intercom buzzed and Marco moved away from her. "I don't mind getting caught in bed with you, but I don't relish being found in the middle of lovemaking." His smile turned rueful. "I lose my control with you, *cara*." He looked utterly mystified by the thought.

She couldn't stop herself from openly admiring his naked body as he strode across the room and picked a pair of well-worn denim jeans from the closet. She watched him slide them up his legs and over his tight rear end. Knowing he wasn't wearing underwear was going to kill her at some point today.

She'd assumed that making love with Marco might take the edge off her desire. She'd been very wrong. Now that she knew what he could make her feel, now that she knew that every promise his sensual lips made, all the dark sexuality his lithe body proclaimed, was understated when compared to the fulfilled promise, she could think of nothing else but tasting him again.

Now that she'd discovered sex, she wondered how in the world people got anything done. That was why, she reasoned, people were so obnoxiously cheerful and scatterbrained at the beginning of an affair. Because good sex scrambled your thoughts and plastered a goofy grin on your face you couldn't erase.

She looked at her reflection in the vanity mirror that was positioned across the room. She definitely had the goofy grin. Her skin was red from the scrape of his whiskers against her delicate face and throat. She knew that if she examined her inner thighs she'd find the same sort of burns. *That* made her blush to the roots of her hair.

She slipped out of the bed and contemplated taking a chance on going to the bathroom to find her suitcase. She hadn't unpacked yesterday. She'd been resigned to sleeping on the couch, and the idea of hanging her clothing in the same closet as Marco's had seemed like an intimacy too far. Which was just about laughable at this point, since there weren't any physical intimacies left—not any that *she* knew about—that she hadn't shared with Marco the night before.

Marco walked back into the room at that moment, shirtless and carrying a tray laden with pastries, fruit and meat. He was every woman's fantasy.

She leaned over and snatched up the sheet in a belated attempt to cover herself.

He laughed and shook his head before setting the tray down on the foot of the bed. He gripped the edge of the sheet and unwound it, leaving her exposed again. He pressed a soft kiss to her lips that left her knees weak.

"No need for you to cover up. I much prefer you naked." He brushed a swath of blond hair out of her face. "You look so much softer."

She looked pointedly at the hard cut of the muscles on his torso. "I can't say the same."

"Yes, but that's one of the many wonderful things that are different about men and women. Our differences complement each other."

A small smile tugged at her lips. "I hadn't thought of it that way before."

"Hungry?" he asked, sitting on the bed and gesturing to the tray.

"Starving." She joined him on the bed, still undressed, wondering where the fleeting moment of sanity she'd had when she'd woken up had gone off to. She felt that silly grin spread across her face again as she looked at the handsome face of her lover. *Her lover.* The grin widened and she knew she looked like the cat that had gotten into the cream and licked the bowl clean. "What's on the menu?"

"Guava, French toast and fresh fruit. And I think that's Spam." He gestured to the pink square slices of meat that were fanned out on the silver tray.

"You're kidding?"

"It's a local favorite."

"I'll pass." She reached over and picked up a slice of mango.

It felt ridiculously decadent, sitting on the bed with him and sharing a tray, eating with their fingers. When he slipped a bite of guava between her lips and lapped up the juices that dribbled down her chin, the entire breakfast, and any resolve she might have hoped to claim, disintegrated.

After they'd made love they went to separate showers to prepare for the day. Marco had tried to cajole her into his, but she knew that she would give in to the temptation of his naked body and they would end up cloistered in the villa all day. Her body was more than willing to take that option, but she felt she needed to get a grip on the situation, and she wouldn't be doing that if she kept allowing Marco to turn her brain to mush with his expert hands and mouth.

She rummaged through her suitcase and found a pair of white linen shorts and a spring green halter-top made of a slithery, silky material that felt decadent against her bare skin. She had never been so aware of her body before last night, before Marco had shown her what it meant to be a woman. She found she didn't want to blend in with the boys anymore. She wanted to celebrate her femininity, embrace the power of it.

Giddiness fizzed in her veins as she quickly tied back her wavy hair and walked out into the main living area of the villa. "So, what's on the agenda?" she asked.

Marco looked up, and was momentarily frozen by the pang of lust that hit him square in the gut and the swelling of emotion that tightened his chest. She looked so young, so vibrantly beautiful. All of her haughty, don't-touch-me demeanor had faded, giving way to a soft, well-loved expression. She looked like a thoroughly satisfied woman, and he couldn't help but glory like a caveman over the fact that he'd been the man, the *only* man, to make her feel that way. He had brought her to the pinnacle of pleasure and caught her as she fell. He had been the only man to kiss her lush breasts, to join his body to hers. The novelty of it was extraordinary. No, he wouldn't even call it a novelty; it was much more than that.

He still had no idea what her game was—if there *was* a game. For the first time he considered that she might be everything she claimed to be. That she wanted her father's company out of a sense of pride and fairness—that she'd entered into their marriage with all her cards laid out on the table. That she had slept with him because she desired him. It hardly made sense, but then it had never mattered one way or the other to him if he understood the inner workings of his mistress's minds. He enjoyed their bodies, but as for their shallow dreams and desires he couldn't have cared less.

Elaine should be no different. She was his wife—*that* was different—but the marriage was nothing more than a business contract. Their proposed affair was an entirely different matter. It was strictly physical, and if Elaine had designs on making the arrangement permanent, or on scamming him out of his vast fortune, she was sadly out of luck. He wasn't the type of man to be bewitched by sex, even if it was fantastic sex. His emotions and his mind always stayed separate. There was absolutely no way Elaine could ensnare him.

"Business." He flashed her a grin and was gratified to see her cheeks turn rosy pink. She still blushed like an innocent, and in spite of himself he found he enjoyed it fully. "I have a meeting with James to discuss my business plan for the resort."

The look of undisguised longing in her eyes—not when she looked at him, but when he mentioned a business meeting—nearly made him laugh. "Would you like to join us, Elaine?"

A sparkle caught in her blue eyes, and he tried to ignore the surge of satisfaction her happiness gave him. "Well, if you wouldn't mind…"

"It's in the bag," Elaine said confidently as they left James's office later that afternoon.

Marco took in her confident smirk with great amusement. "You think so?"

She nodded vigorously, freeing tendrils of hair from her ponytail and bringing them down to frame her face. "Your figures were astounding, not to mention accurate. From what you said in the meeting I can see that your plans will up the revenue by thirteen percent in just two years."

"That's a more generous figure than I had calculated."

"Oh, good—then you hadn't thought of this," she said, almost gleefully. "The very new upscale nightclub you're planning to build on the property can bring in profit from patrons of other hotels and resorts. You don't have to open it to everyone, but making it more inclusive will certainly help it pay for the expense of building it and then some."

"It's definitely a thought."

"It's a good one."

She leaned into him, and the intoxicating scent of her assaulted his senses. He'd had her this morning but his body still felt deprived of her softness, of the fulfillment he'd experienced with her.

"You're very certain of yourself." He leaned in too, and pressed a kiss to her neck, enjoying the little shiver that racked her body.

"You should know that confidence is the key to success," she said breathlessly.

"I thought it was image."

A tortured groan escaped her lips. "I can't remember with you touching me like that!"

"Like this?" He kissed the curve of her neck again.

"Yes. Like that."

"I think it's time to go back to the villa."

"I agree."

The next few days passed in a kind of sensual haze. The sale of the resort was nearly finalized, and James had commanded that Marco take the weekend to romance his wife. In Elaine's opinion, he'd done a pretty good job of it. Breakfast in bed, intimate candlelit dinners, and of course amazing sex. She wouldn't let herself think of it as making love. It was too dangerous. Almost as dangerous as when Marco held her hand during a walk on the beach, or when he held her tenderly against his chest while they were in bed, his arms cradling her close to his body.

Monday morning she expected Marco would be back to business as usual, so it was a surprise when he exited the bathroom wearing a pair of shorts and a threadbare T-shirt. "I thought we would spend the day together," he said. "Did my PA happen to buy you a pair of hiking boots?"

She tried, and failed, to quash the giddy sensations that were fluttering through her. For all she knew his taking time out of his busy schedule to spend with his mistresses was perfectly normal.

The term brought her up short. Was she his mistress? No. She most certainly wasn't. They were equals in their relationship. She wasn't dependent on him, and she certainly wasn't expecting to be a kept woman. She had a job, and her ambitions extended far beyond that.

"I don't think I have hiking boots. I have a pair of tennis shoes, though."

"That should be good enough. You don't get seasick, do you?"

"I have no idea."

His teeth flashed bright white against his tan skin and she felt her limbs go slack. "You're going to find out today."

A slim stream of white sand backed by thick foliage came into view. Elaine leaned over the railing of the small yacht to try and get a better view of their destination.

She inhaled the salt air and was thankful, again, that she apparently didn't suffer from seasickness. The yacht cut through the water like a hot knife through butter, the waves parting and giving deference to the bulk of the sleek ship, which virtually eliminated the feeling of being on water.

Marco walked up behind her and cocooned her in his

firm embrace. "This is the island of Kapu. It means for-bidden, or taboo." The wicked words sent a shiver down her spine. "It's for sale, and I'm considering purchasing it and building a luxury villa on the grounds. It's the ultimate vacation rental. A private island."

"You're going to buy an island?" There was simply no pre-tending to be nonchalant over this extravagant show of wealth.

"It's a lovers' paradise. The fantasy of being the only two people on earth realized, with all of the modern luxuries you could ever want."

She could imagine it all too easily. She and Marco marooned on an island, with nothing more pressing to do than give each other pleasure. She bit back a moan. "So you're thinking of it as an extension of the resort?"

"In a sense. But it will be kept separate, in that only staff and invited guests will be allowed on it when it's in use."

"That sounds…decadent."

He chuckled—his hot breath warming her down to her toes, the sound of his laugh rumbling through her body.

"That's the idea."

It didn't take long for Marco and the small crew to bring the ship into the floating marina. He moved like a man who had been born at sea, his movements sure and swift, his deft fingers tying knots with ease.

"Did your family sail often?" she asked, keeping her eyes trained on the shifting muscles in his forearms as he worked.

He stopped and straightened, a shadow passing over his handsome face. "No." He crossed the deck and climbed up onto the ship's railing before dropping down onto the dock.

She moved to follow him and he stretched his arms up, preventing her from hitting the wooden planks with the force that he had done. "You just seem like a seasoned pro."

Marco never talked about his family, and up until that point she'd thought it might have been an oversight. She should have realized that Marco didn't commit oversights. His avoidance of the subject was very purposeful, and if he didn't want to share the reasons there would be no persuading him. She had been right when she'd guessed that he wasn't a pillow-talker. He wasn't that much of a talker full-stop—not about anything personal—which had suited her fine since she didn't exactly want to rehash *her* disaster of a childhood either. But now it didn't seem enough to limit conversation to the weather and the stock market. She wanted more. And that was very, very dangerous.

"I bought my first boat when I was nineteen. Sailed it from Puerto Vallarta to San Diego and then had it transported across the country. Money was no object," he said ruefully. "I enjoyed it very much."

She could just imagine him on board a sleek white yacht, with women in scanty bikinis draped across the deck…and across Marco. Unbidden, a flame lit in the pit of her stomach. She knew Marco had an unfathomable amount of experience compared to her, and generally she could let it go, but she would be a liar if she claimed it didn't bother her. The thought of other women touching him made her stomach churn.

"I sold it a few years ago," he continued, "because I no longer had the time to take extended boating excursions."

"Cut into your social life?" she snapped, the image of beach beauties pawing at him still at the forefront of her mind.

He gave her a withering glare. "I don't sleep with every woman I'm photographed with."

She tried to look casual at his admission. "Oh?"

"I think you are jealous, *cara mia.*" He looked very entertained by the notion. And, worse still, he was right.

"And my being with other men wouldn't bother *you*?"

He stepped nearer to her and claimed her mouth in a fiery kiss. When they parted their breathing was labored, their heartbeats erratic and audible in the near silence that surrounded them. "They would not live to taste your sweet lips. I would not allow it."

She tried to think of a tart comeback, something pertaining to his origins in the Neolithic era, but every fiber of her being was too busy basking in the pure pleasure of knowing that Marco wanted her and wanted no one else to have her, that he felt possessive of her in the same way she felt possessive of him.

Forsaking all others.

She quickly shook off the remembered snippet of her wedding vows and followed Marco from the dock to the pristine white sand beach. There were no footprints to mar its natural beauty, only gentle, sloping waves caused by the coastal winds.

"I'm told that back in the jungle there's a natural waterfall, if you're up for a walk."

"Most definitely," she said, keeping pace with him as he walked into the thick trees.

To think that only a week ago she'd been sitting in her gray cubicle, crunching numbers. It seemed another lifetime away. She could hardly reconcile the two points of her existence, and yet they were both real.

They moved through the sun-dappled undergrowth, vines reaching out and grabbing them around the ankles every so often. "We need a machete," she grumbled as she tripped over a wayward root.

He turned and quirked a grin at her. "Just a little bit farther. I can hear the water running."

They followed the sound until the treeline ended and

they were standing in a grassy clearing. A waterfall was spilling down a lava rock formation and into a clear pool of deep water.

Marco came to stand beside her, his arm wrapped around her waist, the heat of his body seeping through her clothes, warming her from the inside out.

"This almost doesn't seem real," she breathed. "It's like a fantasy." And she didn't only mean the scene; the man was included as well.

"Do you think it will appeal to those seeking a romantic hideaway?"

"I'd say it's absolutely perfect."

"Want to test the water out?"

She eyed him skeptically. "I thought we were here for business."

Marco felt himself grow hard as he thought about getting her in the water, her body slick, her nipples beaded tight from the coolness of the natural pool.

"We're here to test out the facilities," he said sagely. "I never buy a car without test driving it first. I'm not going to buy an island without sampling some of its attractions."

An impish grin lit her face and she untied the flimsy strings of her halter-top. The close-fitting top had been tormenting him all morning. She pulled the silky shirt over her head and revealed a skimpy electric-blue bikini that barely concealed the fullness of her curves. Her nipples were hard and pressing tightly against the Lycra. He ached to touch her, taste her, to lave his tongue over the small raspberry buds until she cried out for fulfillment.

"See something you like?" she asked.

"I don't know. Keep going."

She rolled her eyes at him and pushed the khaki shorts she was wearing down her long, shapely legs. The bottom to the bikini was just as tiny and insubstantial as the top, the tight blue fabric hugging the round curve of her bottom and revealing hints of peachy flesh.

Her irises expanded, obscuring the color in her eyes, as her body responded to his blatant appraisal of her. "Your turn," she said, her voice taking on the husky quality that he knew signaled her arousal.

She watched as he stripped down to his swim-trunks, her eyes roaming over him with unconcealed desire. She was an anomaly when compared to any of the other women he'd known. She didn't lower her lashes coyly, but neither was her look one of bold invitation. There was nothing contrived in her response. She had such total honesty in her desire. She wanted him, and she did nothing to hide that fact from him, but neither did she strut around like a cat in heat to try and gain his attention.

The pure need in her soft blue eyes was his undoing every time. He hooked his arm around her waist and drew her into his body. Shy excitement lit her face. It amazed him every time she blushed. A surge of emotion caught him off guard, and despite being on solid ground he had the strangest sensation of being unsteady.

He gripped her tightly and took two big steps to the edge of the water before jumping in and submerging them both in the aquamarine depths.

She came up sputtering, her blond hair plastered to her face. She moved the curtain of hair aside and gave him her best evil eye. His charming grin undid her, and all her pique was forgotten. She registered the heat of his skin, warming her in the cool water, the strength of his body as he held her locked against his hard, muscular chest. If she'd been standing her knees would have buckled.

She slithered out of his grasp, submerging herself again,

and swam to the waterfall, aware that he was following behind her, feeling a primitive feminine thrill over being pursued. She climbed up onto a rock that rose out of the pool at the base of the waterfall and sat down on the moss-carpeted surface, curling her legs beneath her.

Marco hoisted himself from the water and onto the rock with ease, his muscles bunching and shifting beneath his tan skin. Slick moisture pooled at the apex of her thighs, but it had nothing to do with the waterfall and everything to do with the supremely gorgeous man who was moving toward her, his dark eyes blazing with intent.

"Pouting?" he asked, trailing his finger along the line of her collarbone.

The contact was almost innocent, yet it made her thoughts turn wanton and wicked.

"Yes, well, you got me wet."

His eyes flickered. "Careful, a man could let that go to his head."

He moved his finger, dipping in the valley between her breasts. She gasped. "Is it always about sex with you?"

"Not always. But when I'm with you that seems to be the subject more often than not." He cupped her breasts, teasing the straining peaks with the pads of his fingers. She shuddered.

She flicked a glance at the dense jungle, looking for any signs of movement in the thick growth of plants. "Marco, we're right out in the open." She couldn't summon enough conviction to give her scolding any weight.

"It's a private island. And the crew is still aboard the yacht."

He leaned in and pressed a kiss to the curve of her neck. Her body went slack, leaning into his, surrendering to the feelings he aroused in her so effortlessly.

He untied the strings on her daring bikini, the one that she'd vowed never to wear on her first inspection of her new wardrobe, and left her bare to his hungry gaze.

He groaned. "You're so gorgeous." He moved his thumb over her tight nipple and she squirmed. She wondered if anyone had ever died from longing, from wanting a man so much it took the breath right from her body.

He moved his hand beneath the falls and let water pool in his palm. Then he brought his hand to her and tilted it slightly over her, let the water trickle slowly over her flesh, so it trailed down the dips and swells of her body, over her already aching breasts. The contrast of concentrated drops of cool water on her overheated skin made her gasp. It also wrenched her arousal up another untenable notch.

She reached behind her head, feeling for something to grip, something to keep her rooted to the earth. She found a fern frond and grasped it in her hands, holding it so tightly that the leaves bit into her palms.

He gathered more water in his hand, tormenting her again with the sharp chill as he let it fall in beads over her bare breasts, this time lapping up the drops with his tongue. She arched into him, begging him silently to possess her, to fill her and take them both to the heights they so desperately craved.

He leaned in and drew her nipple into his hot, moist mouth, and she let out a shocked cry that was swallowed up by the roaring of the water. She released her hold on the plant and gripped the back of Marco's head, holding him to her, needing him to stop for fear that she would shatter, needing him to go on forever, needing to keep experiencing the wicked sensations that were coursing through her body.

He escaped her hold and untied the flimsy bikini

bottoms, his dark eyes turning black with the force of his desire as he looked at her naked body.

"I'm at a disadvantage," she said. She was almost shocked by her growing boldness as she gripped his aroused length through the thin fabric of his swim-shorts. She squeezed him, loving the look of surrender that passed over his handsome face.

She put a hand in the center of his chest and gently shoved him back, moving his shoulders beneath the cascading water. She moved her hands over his bare chest, sliding her fingertips over his slick bare skin.

She hooked her fingers into his shorts and pulled them down his legs, smoothing her hands up his muscled thighs, skimming the area around his erection. His shaft jerked at the near contact and she thrilled at his response. She would never, ever get enough of his body. She would never tire of looking at him. He was the perfect example of what a man should be. Hard, hot, rough and smooth.

She leaned over and took the tip of him into her mouth. He gripped her hair, weaving his fingers into the wet strands. She didn't know if he meant to pull her away or keep her there, but when she slid her lips down over his full length his hand froze, his grip tightening, whatever his original intention had been lost.

She pleasured him that way until his thighs began to quiver beneath her hands, and then he pulled her away, bringing her up the length of his body and taking her mouth in a fierce, deep kiss. When he broke the kiss his breathing was labored, his eyes dark with intensity.

"Was that okay?" she asked.

"Okay?" A strained chuckle escaped his lips. "Any more and this would have been over before it started."

He settled her onto his lap, so that she was straddling

them. The water was showering them both, but doing nothing to cool their mutual desire. He lifted her and settled her onto his erection, gently sliding into her damp core, stretching her, filling her.

He cursed, and she cut him off by pressing her lips to his, absorbing his masculine groan of ecstasy as she began to move.

She rode him, their eyes locked, their breathing fractured. She felt the onset of her climax, but it felt like too much too soon, as though her body couldn't possibly contain it. He moved his hand between them and rubbed her clitoris. She shattered. She screamed, not caring if anyone heard, not mindful of anything but the intense, pulsing sensation that was centered at her apex of her thighs and radiating out through her whole body, filling her so completely that she thought she might burst with it.

Marco thrust hard into her one last time and followed her over the edge, his harsh groan of completion shifting something inside her chest.

He rested his head against her breasts, his arms holding her tightly to him. She cradled his head, holding him to her, craving his closeness to a degree that frightened her.

She had been foolish to believe that she could conduct this affair as if it was business. She would never be free of him after this. He was part of her, in her. He'd changed her.

She had done exactly what she'd been so determined not to do—what she'd thought she would be incapable of doing. She'd committed the unpardonable sin. She had fallen in love with her husband.

CHAPTER NINE

"You're in the mood for Spam this morning?" Marco asked incredulously.

Elaine swallowed the bite she'd been working on and shrugged. "It looked good. Very salty," she said, taking another bite and relishing the flavor. She'd declined the local favorite every other morning during their breakfast in bed sessions, but this morning it had looked mouth wateringly amazing.

They'd been in Hawaii for nearly a month. The sale of the resort had been finalized, and Marco had been working on negotiating a deal for the island of Kapu. Her face, and other parts of her, heated as she thought of the afternoon they'd shared on the forbidden island, making love beneath the waterfall.

The days since then, since the realization that she loved him, had been a sweet kind of torture. On the one hand she felt more alive, more inspired than ever before. She felt things more deeply; her mind was more attuned to the things around her. On the other hand it nearly broke her heart every time she looked at his impossibly gorgeous face and realized that their relationship had a timer ticking on it.

She looked at the plate in front of her and was shocked

to see that she'd polished off more than her share of their breakfast. She gave him a sheepish grin. "I guess I was hungry."

Marco dropped a kiss on her nose and a strange, hot, melting sensation flowed through her body, weakening her limbs. "Sex burns a lot of calories. At least if you do it right. Which we most definitely do."

In spite of the fact that she'd shared every intimacy with him, she blushed. "I can't argue with you." She reached for the remaining piece of meat on their shared plate.

"Plans for the day?" he asked.

Because their "honeymoon" had gone on for so long, she'd been working remotely, doing the accounting for her firm, and she'd continued to actively work on her own business plan.

"No. I finished approving payroll last night while you were at your meeting."

"Excellent. I have to meet with Mr. Naruto briefly this morning, to discuss a final price for Kapu, but after that we can spend the day together."

A sweet feeling of absolute contentment stole over her, leaving her fuzzy. If she could pause everything right then, and just live in this stolen piece of time, she thought at that moment that she would. And that desire frightened her a lot less than it should.

"I might head into town for some supplies," she said.

"You could have the concierge send over whatever you need."

"I know, but then what else am I going to do? I'm not comfortable lying back and being served—especially not when I'm more than capable of going to a grocery store."

Marco could only stare at her determined face. Not a

single one of his ex-mistresses would have opted to run menial errands when they could have been sunbathing or shopping for a designer wardrobe.

His chest tightened. He didn't want to admit that Elaine was in any way different from his other mistresses. He didn't want to admit that she was touching him, thawing some of the hardened, ice-encrusted edges of his heart.

He clenched his fist and turned away from the woman on the bed. She was a hundred times more deadly than the air-headed gold-diggers he'd dated in the past. Because Elaine Chapman's beauty was mixed with a keen mind and a driving ambition that nearly matched his own. The connections their marriage could afford her were limitless. A merger with his corporation once she was at the helm of Chapman Electronics would be priceless. She had to know those things, and while it was easy for him to drop his guard when they were together, when she was offering to do down-to-earth things like grocery shopping it was of the utmost importance for him to remember that her highest goal was power.

Her brand of potent, innocent sexuality made it easy to forget to remain on his guard. But he had to wonder if she was using her innocence to her advantage as well. She was a smart woman, and she certainly wasn't ignorant of the way men viewed a woman's virginity. Perhaps it had seemed advantageous for her to give it to him, for her to use it to make him feel bonded to her? And he'd been allowing her to do that—allowing her to meld herself into his life.

Callous as it sounded, he didn't typically share a room with his women if a trip were going to last so long. He valued his space, his privacy, far too much, and he certainly didn't want to give a woman the wrong idea. But he had dropped his guard with Elaine, and it was a mistake he couldn't continue making.

Marco strode across the room and began to dress. Elaine had seen the shutters come down over his dark eyes, but she couldn't for the life of her figure out what had caused it.

Shrugging off the chill, she rose from the bed and chose her clothing before going into the bathroom to shower. When she surfaced, Marco was gone. His not saying goodbye hurt far worse than she should allow it to.

PMS. That was her excuse for being such an emotional wreck. She'd taken her first blank pill last night, and she was due to start her period any moment. Her body ran like clockwork, thanks to the miracle of her birth control pills, and she no longer had to deal with debilitating cramps and a cycle that ran on a timetable all its own.

She went to the bathroom to prepare for the impending event and was brought up short by the fact that she hadn't started yet. Not even spotting. She placed a hand on her abdomen, expecting at least a slight ache—something to signal the arrival of her period. There was nothing.

With shaking hands she put the necessary items in her purse and made her way out of the villa. She would start soon. Any moment. She had to. Because if she didn't that meant she'd broken a binding part of their agreement.

She slid behind the wheel of the car and tried to ignore the pounding of her pulse. She wasn't pregnant. There was no way. She was on the pill.

The refrain repeated in her mind as she drove the car down the winding road and into town, stopping at the nearest department store.

No way. Not pregnant.

She made a pitstop in the restroom, hoping that nature would grant her a definitive sign that she had not conceived Marco's baby. Still nothing. But it was too early to panic.

Yes, her body had run like clockwork, nearly to the hour, for the last five years, but that didn't mean that there was a baby.

Not pregnant.

Numbly, she moved through the store and into the family planning aisle, pausing at a box of condoms that seemed to mock her with their promise of a ninety-nine percent success rate, and stopped finally in front of a wall of products she'd never looked at in her life. Pregnancy tests.

She placed her hand on her stomach, almost expecting it to be rounded. She began to shake as she examined the boxes. Digital readouts. Early results. Traditional lines. In the end she grabbed three different brands and hurried to checkout, trying to look as nonchalant as possible about buying potentially life-altering items.

With her bag gripped tightly to her chest, she raced out to the parking lot and into the car. She gripped the steering wheel, trying to still the tremors that were racking her body. She couldn't be pregnant. It was a coincidence that she happened to be late for the first time in her memory. After becoming sexually active. A coincidence.

That was what she told herself during the drive back to the hotel. That was what she told herself when she took all three tests and set them gingerly on the vanity top, too afraid to check the results.

Not pregnant, she begged silently.

Finally she stood and stared down at the tests. Two lines on the first test; the digital test proclaimed "pregnant" in stark black and white; two more bright pink lines stared up at her from the final test. There was no questioning the evidence.

Her knees buckled and she sat down on the toilet, gripping the edge of the countertop to keep herself up and conscious.

For one selfish moment all she could think was that her life was over. She'd lost the company—her driving force, the thing that she'd worked so tirelessly for. She'd signed the prenup, mentally shaking her head as she'd done so over the lunacy of even having to make such a deal when she knew there was no chance Marco would be getting close enough to her to make her pregnant.

A baby. She didn't know anything about babies. She didn't want one. She never had. Yet morally she felt she had no option other than to carry the child. Adoption was a possible solution…

Blinding pain, as real and severe as the shock and fear she'd felt upon reading the positive tests, assailed her as she imagined lying in a hospital bed, sweaty and exhausted from labor, handing a tiny squalling baby over to someone else. Never seeing the baby again.

She couldn't hold back the anguished cry that escaped her lips. She couldn't do that either.

She stumbled into the bedroom and sat on the edge of the bed, her eyes so dry they stung, the tears that would give her relief nowhere to be found.

That was how Marco found her an hour later.

"Did your shopping go well?" he asked.

She didn't respond. She only sat on the edge of bed, her knees folded up to her chest, looking smaller, more fragile than he'd ever seen her. She looked as if she was in shock, her lips chalky white, her eyes glassy.

"Are you all right?" He knelt down in front of the bed and gripped her hands. They were freezing. "Has someone hurt you?" Primitive male anger rushed up inside of him, and he felt capable of destroying whoever had dared lay a hand on her, capable of taking them apart piece by piece.

Her eyes snapped up to meet his. "No. I'm okay." She sounded as though she were trying to convince herself.

"Well, you don't look okay. You look like death warmed over."

A broken laugh escaped her lips. "Just what every woman loves to hear."

"You're avoiding the question," he said tersely, the gnawing fear in his gut making his voice harsher than he'd intended.

"I'm pregnant." Her bald statement fell flat in the heavy tropical air, leaving a thick silence in the room.

"You said you were on the pill." His voice held an air of deadly calm—much more terrifying than if he'd started shouting.

"I am. I haven't missed one. I don't know…I don't know how it happened." She looked up into his eyes. They were cold, flat. Somehow that was worse than the force of all of his rage. Yelling she could fight, but this dead silence, this calm, cold wave of anger, she didn't know what to do with.

"You don't know how it happened?"

"Marco, I swear I didn't plan it. Why would I? Legally I've lost the company now. I'm as shocked as you are. This isn't what I wanted!" she exploded.

His dark brows snapped together. "You don't want the baby?"

"No! I mean, I don't know. I haven't had any time to process this. It changes absolutely everything."

"You put on a very good show, *cara*. But you and I both know this only *benefits* you. Access to my power, my money, for far longer than the twelve months agreed. Child support. The prospect of our union becoming permanent. All things that would be very beneficial to you. Although legally, as you said, that means you forfeit the company. I can't imagine you being a very effective CEO with a baby on your hip."

"You honestly think I planned this? That I planned to conceive your baby?"

"You would hardly be the first woman to try and snare me by using pregnancy. You're simply the first one to succeed."

"How could I have possibly planned for this to happen? I was on the pill."

He waved a hand to silence her. "Perhaps. At the very least I think you planned to find a way to make our arrangement more beneficial to you. Whether you planned on using a baby to accomplish your goal, I don't know. But I've suspected that you had ulterior motives since the moment you stepped into my office proposing marriage."

His words cut through her like a knife. He had suspected her from the beginning? Had there ever been a moment when he'd trusted her? When he'd felt something for her? Anger rushed through her, rescuing her from the flood of tears that were threatening.

"If you suspected that I was nothing but a gold-digger, then what does that make you for conducting a relationship with me?"

"It was not a relationship. It was an arrangement," he spat. He turned away from her, shutting her out, his shoulders rigid, his back straight. "Out of curiosity, what was the going rate for your virginity? A price none of the other men were able to pay but one you thought you would be able to extract from me?" He walked out of the villa, his parting shot hanging in the air.

Violent nausea overwhelmed her and she leaped up from the bed and raced across the room, barely making it to the toilet before being sick. She leaned her head against the cool wood of the vanity and let the first of today's tears roll down her cheeks.

Marco breathed in the heavily perfumed air and nearly gagged on the floral scent. That woman, that *puttana*, had made a fool of him. She had made him feel something for her. And all the time, every single moment, she had plotting against him.

And now she was carrying his child. His *child*.

He had thought he could safeguard himself against anything she was planning, but this... In this she had won, because he would not abandon his child. He would not be an absentee parent. His child would be his focus. He would love him and care for him in a way his own parents had failed to do for him and his younger brother. In that he was absolutely determined.

And he would not let his child's mother leave him. His child would want for nothing, and that included both parents in the same household. And he knew how to ensure that that happened.

He strode back into the villa, his mind absolutely made up.

"Elaine."

She appeared in the doorway of the bathroom a moment later, her face white, a sheen of sweat on her brow. His heart clenched and he hardened it, shunning the tender feelings she still managed to rouse in him.

"There is only one way to solve this."

She put a hand over her stomach. "I'm not giving up the baby."

"I am not asking that of you. We will remain married. It is the only option."

Elation and horror vied for top position inside of Elaine. "What?"

"It is not what I would have chosen, but the simple fact is that I will not be a part-time father. Neither will I deprive a child of his mother. That leaves us with one option."

"Millions of people share custody of their children—"

He cut her off. "I will not be one of them. It is never in a child's best interest to be treated as though they are an incidental. My own parents could not be bothered. My father threw us out onto the street—my mother, my brother and myself—when I was just twelve. After a couple of years of scraping by and living in homeless shelters my mother met a wealthy man who did not want children, so she left us to fend for ourselves while she pursued a life of luxury. I will never let a child of mine go through life feeling so insignificant. I will never subject my own flesh and blood to that kind of indifference."

The charity for homeless children and Marco's passion for the cause, his reluctance to mention his family, suddenly made horrifying sense. He had been homeless. Not orphaned. Far worse than that. His parents had been alive and too absorbed in their own vacuous existence to worry about the survival of their children.

Her heart ached for the boy he'd been and the man he had become—a man who could not trust and did not believe in love. Yet how could she blame him? How could she even hold his reaction to her pregnancy against him when she knew what he'd had to endure at the hands of those who should have loved him more than they loved anyone or anything else? She felt his pain as though it were her own, and it destroyed the anger that had been growing inside her.

"If you agree to stay in the marriage I will have a new

contract drafted, guaranteeing you the ownership of
Chapman Electronics plus a generous allowance."

She hadn't forgotten about the company, nor had her
desire for it dissipated in any way, but she wouldn't stay in
the marriage for that reason alone—not when the nature of
their relationship had changed irrevocably; not when she
knew what he thought of her. But knowing what she did now,
about his childhood, about the way he had been forced to
survive on his own, caring for his younger brother, she knew
she could not deny him this chance to have a family, this
chance to repair the things that had been broken in his life.

"I accept," she said, the ridiculously formal words
sounding wrong for the situation.

He laughed cynically. "I had a feeling you would see
it my way."

Her defense caught in her throat, stuck behind a lump
of grief. Her heart felt broken—for him, for herself, for everything they'd shared together. Everything they'd lost.

They flew back to New York the next day. Marco was
silent and avoiding her while burying his head in his work,
and she was trying to do the same. She spent a good portion
of the flight in the bathroom being sick. Her morning
sickness, which did not see fit to limit its active hours to
the morning, had hit with a vengeance once they'd hit the
sky, and it hadn't let up.

When the plane touched down in the city she walked
on wooden legs to the car that was waiting for them and
slid inside. The drive back to the penthouse was as quiet
as the miserable plane ride. Marco hated her. He had
already tried her and found her guilty based on the past
actions of those in his life.

Not that she could blame him. She knew what it was like

to be so shaped by past experience; to carry deeply etched scars inside yourself that were not visible to the naked eye.

Her own life had been one desperate attempt at separating herself from her father's perception of her, from the influence of her mother. She had wanted so much to achieve what her father thought her incapable of, using that drive to steer clear of the self-destructive nature she feared she might have inherited from her mother.

Her mother, who had been so weak, so needy for someone to fill the gap in her life, so desperate for the attention of a husband who did not love her that she had sought solace in the arms of countless lovers in addition to drugs and alcohol. Her mother had self-destructed: a combination of narcotics, a Ferrari and a tree ending her life when she was much too young.

Elaine knew all about the sort of bitterness Marco carried inside him, only his was much worse. At least her father loved her—even if he did try to impose his medieval ideals on her. What Marco had endured was unspeakable, and she knew his scars ran much deeper than hers.

The elevator ride from the bottom floor of the apartment building to Marco's top-floor penthouse left her feeling nauseous. She barely made it into the marble bathroom before losing the measly amount of food she'd managed to choke down during the last leg of the flight.

A warm hand settled on her clammy forehead and she tried to move away, hating that Marco was seeing her huddled up against the toilet, sweating and shaking.

"Is this normal?" he asked, his accent thickened with concern. "It doesn't seem like this can possibly be normal."

"I'm afraid it is. At least, that's what I've heard from female co-workers over the years," she said weakly.

"You must see a doctor. This cannot be good for the baby. You are not getting enough nutrition."

Of course he was concerned for the baby, not for her. Still, pleasure curled at the edges of her heart. He cared about the baby, as she was beginning to. She had been so frightened at first, so unable to believe that she could actually be pregnant, that it had been easy to detach. But now that the symptoms were so pronounced, now that she truly felt different, it was easier to believe, easier to imagine the reality of a child—her child—growing inside of her. It was easier to truly love the small baby that was nestled in the protective embrace of her womb.

"I know." She stood on shaky knees, feeling like a newborn giraffe and certain she looked just as ungainly. "My normal gynecologist is also an OB. I'll give her a call."

"What is her name?" Marco asked, the request more of a demand, coming from his autocratic mouth.

"Dr. Alyssa Calvin."

As soon as she'd blurted out the name Marco had retrieved his phone from his pocket and hit the one on his speed dial.

"Cassie, I need you to phone Dr. Alyssa Calvin and make an appointment for one o' clock today for Mrs. Elaine De Luca." He snapped the phone shut and placed it back in his jacket pocket.

"Marco! What if she has appointments?"

He shrugged. "Not my concern. I happen to be free today, and I want to be present at the appointment."

"What if I don't want you to be there?" she asked, knowing already that the argument was a loss. It would take several fully armed guards to stop Marco when he was on a mission.

"You would have me miss the medical confirmation of

our little miracle?" He regarded her closely, his sexy mouth pressed into a grim line. "Is there a reason for that?"

"Are you implying that I've lied to you about being pregnant?"

"It is not unheard of."

"You think I engineered *this?*" She gestured to the toilet.

"I've known a great many women who could empty their stomach contents on demand."

Rage vibrated through her. "I'm not going to spend the rest of this marriage trying to prove that I'm not plotting against you!"

Anger was replaced by a feeling of crushing defeat, and she swayed on her feet. Marco reached out an arm to steady her, bringing her close to the heat of his body. It was the first time she'd been so close to him since she'd found out about the baby and she melted into him, her body craving the heat from his.

Marco felt wetness from her tears penetrate the fabric of his shirt. Guilt assailed him. He was not a man who allowed uncertainties. He made decisions and he acted on them. He charted a course and he followed it. There was no room for doubt, no room for any sort of confusion. And yet with Elaine he wasn't certain of anything. She could be strong, yet she could also be achingly vulnerable. He wanted to lash out at her, condemn her for what she had done, and yet he also wanted to fold her into his embrace and promise her that everything would be all right.

"I'm sorry, Elaine."

She stiffened in his arms. "For?"

"For what I said a moment ago. I know you did not lie about being pregnant."

She pulled away from him and turned to face the vanity, trying to put her disheveled hair in order. "But you're not sorry for saying I orchestrated the whole thing in the first place?"

"It does seem rather convenient."

She laughed. "Oh, yes, so convenient. The vomiting combined with being married to a man who thinks me so mercenary that I would conceive his baby to get my hands on his cash is about the most *convenient* thing that has ever happened to me." Tears welled up in her blue eyes and spilled down her waxen cheeks.

His heart twisted, the pain from witnessing her anguish was like a physical blow.

He clenched his teeth and hardened himself against the unconscionable swell of emotion.

He turned away from her. "I cannot be manipulated, Elaine. Do not waste your time trying to appeal to my softer side with your tears."

It took every ounce of discipline to leave her standing there, looking shocked and injured, but he could not allow her to affect him. He'd never had trouble keeping his emotions separate from his affairs, and yet he had allowed Elaine to get closer, deeper inside of him, than he had ever allowed another woman to get.

It had been his mistake—trusting her, permitting her to mean something to him. He was not a fool. He had clawed his way up from the depths of poverty, he had built up a billion-dollar industry from nothing, and he would not allow himself to be taken down by a woman.

He would not make the mistake of trusting her again.

CHAPTER TEN

"EVERYTHING looks good, Mrs. De Luca," Dr. Calvin said as she wiped the ultrasound gel from Elaine's stomach. "I'll need to see you again in another month, but until then, unless you have any questions, I think you're free to go."

Elaine opened her mouth to say she didn't have any questions but Marco, who was standing next to the exam room bed, arms folded, looking like some Roman god of thunder, interrupted.

"You are certain that she can continue to work?"

Dr. Calvin gave Elaine an understanding smile before addressing Marco. "She should be able to continue all of her usual activities, within reason."

"But if her work is too stressful…"

"Then give her a foot-rub when she gets home. Really, Mr. De Luca, women have been having babies since the dawn of time. As much as it might feel that way, your wife isn't the first woman to experience pregnancy."

Elaine tried to hide the smile that crept slowly across her face. Marco was looking stormier than he had a moment ago.

It was easy to pretend that he was just like any other

concerned husband, even though she knew that was far from the truth. She was just the vessel to carry his child—the female figurehead who would play the role of mother to his heir. He hated her. He had made it abundantly clear that morning. If he'd experienced a moment of concern over her being sick it was simply because he was worried about the health of the baby.

Yet—silly, stupid woman that she was—she'd soaked in his attentiveness, craving his touch, the feel of his lips on hers. It was humiliating to love him so much when she knew that he would get rid of her if his conscience would allow it. Even more humiliating that she couldn't kill her love for him. And he couldn't kill the love she felt for him either, though he was doing a good job of trying.

When they left the doctor's office Marco's limo was already parked against the curb, waiting for them. Marco let her get in first, and when he sat down she noticed that he kept a long stretch of empty seat between them.

"I have to go to the office now," he said curtly.

"Then I'm going to work too," she said, daring him to disagree. "The doctor said it was fine."

He turned, his dark eyes flashing. "You need rest. You must be jet lagged, and you spent the entire flight being sick."

"I need to check in," she insisted.

"Absolutely not." He leaned forward and pressed the intercom, and spoke in rapid Italian to the driver. He leaned back heavily and pulled his BlackBerry out of his jacket pocket, intent on email and very purposefully ignoring her.

The car pulled up at the De Luca Corporation headquarters and Marco got out with barely a nod of farewell. The slam of the car door expressed the anger he had chosen not to voice.

She leaned back in the seat, fighting the uncharacteristic tears that were threatening to fall again. She *was* tired. She *did* just want to go home and curl up in a ball and sleep. But she was not going to be dictated to, and the sooner Marco realized that the easier life would be.

She pressed the button on the intercom. *"Scusi?"* She knew her Italian was pitiful, but she thought it would be best to at least try.

"Si?" Paolo's muffled voice came over the speaker.

"I've changed my mind. About going home, that is. I need to go to Burke and Black. It's on Sixth."

"Si."

She managed to make it through a half day without falling asleep at her desk, and took the rest of her work back to the penthouse to finish in the comfort of her own bed, with the aid of Chinese takeout.

Paolo, Marco's chauffeur, had made himself available to her when he wasn't shuttling Marco around, and he'd agreed to take her to her favorite Chinese restaurant and then back home.

She'd ordered three extra entrées with the feeble hope that Marco might be home in time for dinner, and that he might join her. Both desires seemed to be unlikely, but she was always painfully hopeful when it came to Marco.

Any normal person would be angry with him for the assumptions he'd jumped to, but it was becoming clear to her that when it came to Marco her emotions defied logic. There was some anger, but mostly she just ached for the boy who had grown up with no one to show him what true, unselfish love was, and for the man he had become—the man who couldn't trust anyone for fear of being hurt again.

She'd been hurt. Her own family had been a dismal example of suburban dysfunction, and she'd let that affect her. She'd also allowed what had happened with Daniel to halt her dating career. But none of those things mattered. Not now. She was making a new life with Marco, with their child. She was determined it would be a good life, better than the childhood either Marco or herself had experienced.

Finding out she was pregnant had been the single most terrifying thing that had ever happened to her, but after going to the doctor, after seeing the little barely formed shape on the ultrasound screen, she knew she wanted her baby. She knew she loved her baby.

She didn't know where the company would fit in yet. It still mattered—she'd worked her whole adult life at becoming qualified and finding a way to take over Chapman Electronics. But the baby had to come first. On that point both she and Marco were in total agreement.

Her stomach was begging for nourishment before she finally gave in and ate, abandoning the idea of a nice dinner together. She ate the Chinese food with none of the relish that she normally felt. It all just seemed bland without him.

She opted against working in her room, and spread all her documents out on the coffee table in her usual organized disaster. She tried to pretend she wasn't watching the clock and listening for the sound of the elevator moving between floors.

The overwhelming pull of exhaustion finally won out over her desire to be awake when Marco arrived home and she fell asleep on the couch, her work still spread over her lap.

The pinging of the lift doors jerked her out of her sleep. "Marco?"

He moved stiffly from the entry to the living area, his jaw tight, his eyes flat and unreadable. "You should be in bed."

"I was working and I fell asleep." She stretched, trying to get the kinks worked out of her joints.

"You need your rest," he said curtly. "This isn't good for the baby."

"There's leftover Chinese food in the fridge," she said, ignoring his autocratic statement.

"I already ate."

It hurt her that he'd had dinner without her, without even letting her know. It was a small, stupid thing, but in Hawaii, before she'd found out about the baby, they'd shared every meal together. Her face heated as she remembered the time they'd shared a mango at the private beach, and he'd let the juices of the sweet fruit drip down her chin before licking away the stickiness.

The face of the man standing before her and the face of the man in her memory were impossible to meld together. The man from the beach was a fantasy—her lover, her friend. This man was a cold, remote stranger.

She stood and took a step toward him. He turned away and began to move in the direction of his office. "I have more to do," he said by way of explanation. "I'll be leaving early for work, so I doubt we will see each other in the morning. Get some rest."

He left her standing there, her arms wrapped around herself, trying to hold in what body heat she had left, trying not to give in to the misery that was filling her entire being.

Marco managed to completely avoid her over the next week. He spent most of his time at the office, and when he wasn't there he was in the home office. She wanted nothing more than to close the ever-widening gap that had opened up between them, but he seemed determined to speak as few words to her as possible. He only ever talked to her to ask about her health, and that was out of concern for the baby.

She looked at the clock that hung on the wall of her cubicle. It was pushing nine o'clock and she was still at work. All of her co-workers had left hours ago, and she was still sitting, alternating between quadruple-checking that week's time card and adding up some data projections for Chapman Electronics. She didn't want to go home and face Marco's chilly silence. It was always painful, but she was even more aware of his rejection when they were both in the same space.

Finally, at ten, she knew that she couldn't avoid the penthouse any longer. Marco was likely to be cloistered in his office by now anyway, pretending she didn't exist. Her heart clenched.

By the time she made it back home she felt ready to fall asleep standing up. She'd had to take a cab home, which she didn't like to do, but she'd liked the prospect of walking home in the dark, almost overcome by exhaustion, even less. The lift doors swung open and she stumbled into the living room, fatigue slowing her movements.

Marco was standing by the bar in the living room, his expression dark. He brought the tumbler of Scotch in his hand down onto the marble bar with a crack. "Where have you been?"

"Work," she said, trying to sound flippant.

"Tell me, *cara mia*, how will you bleed me for child support if you drop dead from exhaustion before you are able to collect it?" He crossed the room in long strides.

Were it any other man he might have frightened her, but she knew that Marco would never harm her, no matter how angry he was.

"The doctor said going to work was fine. I don't have to take orders from you."

"No, but you might want to try and engage some common sense."

"It isn't as though I was out running the New York Marathon! Sitting behind a desk isn't likely to put me at any great risk!" Her tiredness began to ebb as adrenaline surged through her veins.

"Is that what you were doing? Because I've had hours to put together all the possible scenarios for how you were spending your time. You could have been injured. Something might have happened to the baby."

He was leaning close to her now, the spicy scent of his cologne teasing her nostrils, reminding her of forbidden pleasures. Pleasures that seemed as though they were from another lifetime.

"You could have been in the hospital, or worse, and you didn't even afford me a courtesy call to let me know you would be late. Your office phone rang straight to voicemail, and you didn't have your mobile on you either, so I had no way of reaching you." His dark eyes were blazing with more heat than she'd seen in over a week.

"I…I'm sorry. I didn't want to worry you." That much was true. She hadn't really imagined that Marco would care where she was. He seemed content to avoid and ignore her when they were in the same vicinity, and she certainly hadn't envisioned him pacing the floor in concern over finding her missing.

"Anything could have happened to you!" he said roughly. He stroked his thumb over her tender lower lip. "I pictured you lost. Hurt. I could not reach you. You cannot do that to me again."

He hooked an arm around her waist and leaned in,

claiming her mouth hungrily, desperately, his tongue plundering the depths of her mouth, his lips moving furiously over hers.

She was helpless to do anything but submit to his passion. She wrapped her arms around his neck, pouring every ounce of the frustration that had been building over the past few days into the kiss.

Marco drew Elaine hard against the length of his body and pressed his erection firmly against her. Let her feel what she did to him, what he was powerless to control.

Rage had reached boiling point, turning to passion, desperation. He forked his fingers through her mass of blond hair and began to press hot open-mouthed kisses to her neck, her collarbone, the faint shadow of cleavage that was just barely hinted at by her demure blouse.

When he'd returned home and found her gone he had imagined her leaving, returning to her old apartment, or simply disappearing. It had gutted him. Utterly. Completely. He had imagined never seeing his child, not being able to care for him, raise him. He had promised himself that if he were to ever have children their care would be his top priority. He had imagined losing that chance. Imagined having his child grow up believing his father did not care.

And he had imagined never seeing Elaine again. Never kissing her soft lips or sinking into her warm, willing body—never having her legs wrapped around him again as she cried out his name in ecstasy.

She would not leave. He knew she wouldn't. There would be no way for her to collect her precious company if she did that. And yet old fears had claimed him, images of being left, of feeling stranded and utterly, completely alone.

It's because of the child.

If not for the baby the gold-digger could go and latch

onto any other man she pleased. What he felt for her was all about sex and lust. He should not want her as he did—not knowing what she was. And yet he was a slave to his passion for her. At this moment he could no more deny himself her body than he could deprive himself of oxygen.

"I need you," she whispered, her voice broken, her body trembling.

"I need you too, *bella. Amore mia.*" He deftly unbuttoned her shirt and parted the fabric, revealing her pearly skin. Her perfect breasts were shielded from him by only the sheerest whisper of lace. "So beautiful."

He swept her up off the floor and carried her down the hall. Her eyes were wide, her kiss-swollen mouth parted in surprise. "I cannot wait," he said. He could hear the torture evident in his own voice.

He laid her down on his bed and knew that he had never seen a lovelier sight than this woman, spread out before him, offering herself to him with total trust, total desire.

He knelt down on the bed and leaned over her, kissing her softly on the lips. She squirmed beneath him. She was hot for him, ready for the next step. But he would make her wait. He would make her feel the desperation that consumed him, make her ache as he did.

His pulse pounded in his head as he undid the front clasp of her bra and pushed the flimsy cups aside, leaving her bare for his inspection. Her rosy pink nipples were puckered, begging for the attention of his mouth.

He swirled his tongue around one tightened bud, careful to avoid the pouting tip. She arched beneath him, her breathing ragged. A low moan escaped her lips as he laved the swollen flesh that surrounded her taut nipple. She bowed off the bed when the tip of his tongue brushed the dusky skin of her areola.

"Marco, I can't wait."

He lifted his head and cupped her chin in his hand. "But the waiting makes it so much sweeter, *cara mia*. I want you to burn for me."

"I do," she whispered, her blue eyes unveiled, the honesty of her words beyond question.

"For me. Only for me."

"Yes, Marco, my love. Please."

He removed his clothing as quickly as his unsteady fingers would allow. He joined her on the bed, bare skin to bare skin. He flicked open the closure on her pants and slid them down her shapely legs, taking her filmy panties with them and consigning them to the floor with the rest of their clothes.

He ran a finger up the inside of her thigh and her muscles quivered. "Elaine, *bella*, I would spend all night exploring your lovely body, but I cannot wait to have you."

He parted her thighs and moved between them, placing the tip of his erection at the opening of her slick channel. She gripped his shoulders, her dainty fingernails digging into his skin, the light pain making the blinding pleasure of easing into her tight, wet body almost bearable.

Her short cry of ecstasy and the gentle pulse of her internal muscles as he filled her to the hilt nearly sent him over the edge. He bit back a groan and tensed every muscle in his body, using every ounce of his self-control to keep himself from coming then and there.

Her sweet feminine sighs worked against the last vestiges of his control, shredding it, leaving him exposed. He pumped into her wildly, no longer able to think about making it last, no longer able to think about anything but the roar of ecstasy pounding through his blood, bringing him closer to completion with each stroke.

He felt her muscles clench around him, the rhythmic pulsing signaling her impending orgasm. He thrust into her hard, emptying himself into her, giving himself up to the blinding heat of his climax. She wrapped her legs tightly around his waist and gripped his shoulders, her petite body arching stiffly beneath him as she rode out the wave of her orgasm.

They lay entwined together, their breathing harsh and broken.

She'd called him her love.

He rolled away from her and sat up. His chest suddenly felt too full. He stood and walked into the bathroom, closing the door behind him. He turned the shower on cold and stepped under the harsh spray, trying to numb the conflicting feelings that had invaded his body.

Elaine brought her knees to her chest and tried to still her thundering heartbeat. She closed her eyes and attempted to block out the sound of the shower. The sound of Marco washing her off his skin.

Nausea rolled through her. There was no excuse for the way she'd behaved, for what she'd allowed herself to do. Marco had made his feelings for her plain, and yet she'd still fallen into bed with him at a speed that left her feeling a deep sense of shame.

It hadn't been this way before. She'd known that he hadn't loved her, but he hadn't hated her either. Tonight she had been nothing more than a body to him. Nothing more than a means of finding physical release. He had taken her to bed, joined himself to her in the most intimate way, and he'd hated her the whole time.

She climbed out of his bed and scrambled to collect her clothes. She clenched her hands into fists and tried to stop the uncontrollable shaking that had taken over her limbs. Tears blinded her vision. She hated what she'd allowed herself to do. That she'd let him use her like that—that she'd wanted him to do that to her even knowing how he felt about her.

It would be so easy to blame Marco, but the blame lay with her. She'd let herself become that weak-willed woman she'd hated all of her life.

She didn't know when it had started, but everything in her life now depended on Marco. The fate of the company, her happiness, her self-worth. Everything. She had despised her mother growing up, never understood how she had allowed her father's indifference to destroy her the way it had. She knew how it could happen now. She had been letting it happen to *her*.

Marco didn't love her. He never would. In her pig-headedness she'd imagined making him see her love, making him understand what love was, making him love her in return. It had never occurred to her that it wouldn't work out—not deep down. She, who should have lost every ounce of idealism at the hands of her awful childhood and her initiation into the real world as an adult, had not really believed that her ending would be unhappy.

In a blinding moment of clarity she saw herself in the future as a bitter, unhappy woman, unable to give her child the love and support it needed because she was so wrapped up in contriving ways to gain her husband's affection. An affection she would never be able to earn.

She covered her mouth with her hand to keep a sob from escaping.

She dressed quickly and went back to her own bedroom. She locked the door behind her and slid down the smooth wood, finally letting misery overtake her.

CHAPTER ELEVEN

AT FIVE-THIRTY the next morning she heard Marco's bedroom door open. She hadn't slept at all. She'd been packing. She'd only packed the essentials—nothing that had been purchased with Marco's money. Child support she would accept, but she wasn't going to take anything for herself.

She opened the door and walked slowly out into the kitchen, her shoes loud on the hard floor in the quiet of the morning.

Marco turned, his expression flat, no indication of what had passed between them the night before evident in his dark eyes. "You're up early. Are you feeling well?"

She swallowed, hoping he wouldn't hear the lump in her throat when she spoke. "I'm fine."

He turned away from her and poured a cup of coffee. She couldn't stop herself from drinking in his appearance—his broad shoulders encased in the tailored black suit jacket, his lean waist and hips. She took a breath and winced at the sharp pain that hit her heart. She might never have a chance to just look at him again, to take in all that masculine beauty that would never really be hers.

She took a shuddering breath. "Marco, I want a

divorce." Her words were amplified in the silence of the kitchen.

Marco stilled, his shoulders tightening. He turned toward her, the coffee mug gripped tightly in his fist. *"Che cosa?"* He spat out a tirade of violent Italian. She'd never heard Marco's English desert him before, but at that moment he seemed incapable of using his second language.

"I don't speak Italian," she said quietly.

"And I must not speak English very well," he said, his accent thick, "because I heard you asking for a divorce."

"I did," she said, striving for calm, trying to keep the wobble out of her voice.

"You will not get the company if you leave me. You know that, don't you?"

She blinked furiously. "I understand that. We had a deal, and I'm backing out of it. The terms of the contract are very clear."

She knew she was losing her chance at having the company and, far more painful than that, she was losing Marco, but she had to do it. She couldn't face waking up one day and discovering that she'd lost the essence of who she was, trying to gain the love and affection of a man who would prefer it if she'd never entered his life. The pain, the cost, were simply too great.

"And what about the baby?"

"I'm having the baby. A lot of people share custody of their children, Marco. We can make it work."

His lips went white around the edges and a deadly calm came over him. He turned away from her, as if suddenly he was uninterested in her. "If that is what you want, then of course I will not fight you. I did not want to be married to you any more than you desired to be married to me. I only suggested that we try to make it work for the sake of the baby, and for your own sake. It would have made your life much easier. I will have my lawyer contact yours, and we can discuss a custody arrangement that pleases both of us."

Numbness settled over her. Marco didn't care if she left. Maybe he didn't hate her. Maybe hate was an emotion that was far too passionate for him to bother feeling for her.

"I packed my essentials," she said quietly. "I was going to leave the rest."

"As you wish." He didn't turn to face her again.

"My lawyer will be in touch, then."

Marco made no effort to look at the lying witch's face. *"Si,"* he bit out.

He heard her timid footsteps as she crossed the wood floor and listened for the final click of the elevator doors. Then he threw his mug of coffee at the wall and watched it shatter, the dark liquid staining the pristine white of the wall. He clenched his fists, trying to control the driving need to tear the apartment apart, to make it as broken as everything else in his life. She had been in his bed last night. She had clung to him, dug her nails into his skin, cried out his name in ecstasy as he joined his body to hers. And this morning she had walked out the door without hesitation.

Why would she leave now? Why when she knew she would not get the company? He clenched his jaw. It didn't matter why. It was better that she was gone. Better that she leave now than in ten years. And he had never honestly thought that she would stay. A slow ache grew inside of him and he placed his hand on his chest to try and stanch the flow, shocked at the intensity of the real physical pain that he was feeling.

Yes. It was much better that she was gone now. He had already let her mean too much—had already let her get too far beneath his skin.

At least he had let her go without betraying his pain. He had clung to his mother, begged her not to go. It had made no difference. He would not debase himself like again—least of all for a faithless harlot.

He looked over at his tidy living room; the mess of paperwork that normally cluttered his coffee table was gone. Elaine was gone. He steeled himself against the onslaught of fresh pain that tore at the bloody hole in his chest where his heart used to be.

Elaine sat at her desk, ensconced in the privacy of her cubicle, and stared blankly at the gray walls while her fingers moved over her ten-key on autopilot.

Sometimes a smell or a sound would trigger a memory of her time with Marco, and a pain would assail her that was so swift, so acute, that it nearly made her knees give way.

She blinked. Her eyes felt like sandpaper. She had no more tears left in her after a week of constant crying jags. All that was left now was a deep-seated ache that pervaded her entire being.

"Mrs. De Luca?"

Fresh pain wrenched through her at the sound of her married name. She turned and saw one of the interns standing in her cubicle doorway, a manila envelope in her hand.

"Yes?" Elaine dug her nails into her palms, trying to offset the shooting pain that was racing through her body.

"This came for you just a minute ago."

The girl thrust the envelope into her hand. When Elaine saw the name of Marco's lawyer emblazoned across the top she started to feel dizzy.

The intern bent down in front of her. "Are you all right? You look sick."

Elaine nodded, trying to swallow. "I'm fine."

The girl nodded and left, giving Elaine a concerned, lingering look.

Elaine tore into the package, her fingers trembling. Inside was a very official-looking letter, obviously drafted by Marco. Elaine skimmed it, looking for mentions of the word "divorce".

When she'd finished the missive, her heart was pounding. He had given her the company. No strings. A *gift*. Which was perfectly in keeping with her father's contract. There was nothing that said she couldn't inherit the company, and nothing that said she couldn't receive it as a free gift.

A soft curse escaped her lips and she let the paper in her hand fall to the floor. He'd given her everything but what she wanted most. She just wanted him. It was a bitter moment to discover that the company, her life's ambition, meant absolutely nothing without Marco by her side to share in it with her.

Early Saturday morning Elaine walked through the dimly lit halls of Chapman Electronics and took the elevator to the top floor—to her new office. She still had two weeks left at Burke and Black, and she wasn't about to leave her co-workers in the lurch by leaving without notice.

Her father's former secretary, Lynne, had agreed to come in later that morning and help her get familiarized with the layout of things. Elaine would have to remember to get the older woman a gift for being so nice.

She opened the door to the office and grimaced. It was exactly as she remembered it: stuffed duck mounts frozen in eternal flight on the wall, a dark wooden desk and forest-green carpet. She would change everything about it as soon as possible.

She positioned herself in the wingback chair and laid her head down on the desk, hoping the cold surface would cool her heated skin. She was suddenly very aware that she had no one to share this moment with.

She cradled her flat stomach with her hand. "Well, little one, I made it. Funny thing is it doesn't seem so important anymore." A fat tear slid down her cheek and splashed onto the desk.

She ached for Marco's touch, for the sound of his husky, faintly accented voice, for his presence. She clenched her fist and sat up straight. This was why she'd left in the first place. It wasn't healthy, this obsessive unreturned love. The pain would fade; her feelings would fade. They had to.

She spent the rest of the morning getting to know her father's antiquated filing system with the aid of the ever-helpful Lynne. By lunchtime her stomach was shouting at her to get nourishment quickly, and she'd learned since becoming pregnant that she couldn't ignore hunger pangs when they started gnawing at her.

"I think I'm going to order some Chinese food. Lynne, do you want anything?"

The other woman flushed a bit. "No, I brown bagged. Actually, you have a lunch appointment."

"I do?" Her stomach protested the idea of anything coming between her and her sweet and sour chicken.

"Yes. It's an old appointment, and it couldn't be re-scheduled. You can handle it though. You're a sharp girl."

"Thanks, Lynne. I'd still like to order some Chinese, though."

"I'll take care of it for you," Lynne said, backing out of the office with a smile.

"Sweet and sour chicken, please!" she shouted through the closed door.

For the first time in more than a week the pain her chest had ebbed, replaced by a teeming fleet of butterflies in her stomach that were threatening to demolish her critical thinking skills. She didn't even know what the meeting was about, much less if she was ready for it!

Of course you are! You've been training for this day all of your adult life!

She leaned back in her chair and smoothed her hair down, trying to look cool and professional. She straightened a line of pencils on the desk four different times in an effort to keep her hands busy.

Only five minutes later the door to her office cracked open and the smell of crispy chicken wafted into the room. She pulled her head up sharply and blinked. She'd finally started hallucinating. Because there was no way that Marco was standing in the doorway holding takeout boxes. She had fantasized about him too many times. Had dreamt that he was with her again, in bed, holding her tightly against his body, his heartbeat pounding rhythmically against her back.

"I assume that your craving is still sweet and sour?" He moved into the room, bringing the tantalizing smell of food and the musky, unique scent that was all Marco with him.

She nodded dumbly. "You're my lunch appointment?" She still didn't fully believe that the man standing in front of her was really there.

"Yes. I'm sorry. I asked Lynne to tell a white lie for me."

Which explained why Lynne had looked so sheepish!

"What…what are you doing here?"

"I'm here to see you." He spread his hands apart in a helpless gesture.

"Did you bring your lawyer?"

"I thought it might be best if we talked without legal counsel present." Marco sat heavily in the chair that was placed in front of her desk.

She'd been so bowled over by his presence that she hadn't noticed until just then how worn out he looked, how tired. His lean face looked almost sunken; his golden pallor had an ashen overtone. His normally immaculate hair looked as though he'd run his fingers through it too many times, and the brackets around his mouth looked as if they'd deepened. He looked exactly as she felt. Older. Tired.

Marco looked up, his dark eyes holding a depth of emotion she couldn't fathom. "I want you to come back."

She put a hand to her breast to try and keep her heart from leaping out of her chest. It was her every fantasy come true. Except she had left him, and her reasons for leaving were still sound. She loved him, body and soul, but having that love unreturned would ultimately destroy her.

"I can't, Marco." She formed the words slowly, her mouth rebelling against the order to speak them.

"What is it you need? An allowance? A different home? I can give you whatever you need."

"No. I don't think you can."

He swore violently and stood from the chair. "Do you need me to beg? Because I promised myself I would never lay down my pride like that again. But if that is what it takes to get you to come home to me I will do it and condemn my pride to hell. Please, Elaine. Come home to me."

"Marco…"

"I love you. And I will do whatever it takes to make you love me in return."

Her mouth went completely dry, and it seemed as if the walls of the office, the desk, the chair, everything holding her to the earth had fallen away, leaving only the two of them. "You're just saying that because of the baby," she said hoarsely.

"No. I love our unborn child, but you're the one who has left a gaping hole in my life. I miss your laughter. I miss your wit, your beauty, your body—the mess you leave on my coffee table," he ground out. "I miss your smell, your touch, arguing with you. I miss everything about you, Elaine, and I need you to come home to me. I need you to be my wife in every sense of the word."

Fresh tears welled up in her eyes and she fought to speak around the lump that had formed in her throat. "But you seemed so…indifferent when I left."

"I was an idiot. I was clinging to my pride. I didn't want you to know. I didn't want to face what you had come to mean to me. But I'm done having pride. It means nothing if I cannot have you. I would rather lose everything I have than lose you. I know I said unforgivable things to you when you told me about the baby and I cannot make excuses." He rounded the desk and knelt before her, taking her hands in his. "I can only explain to you what I felt. I felt too much for you—more than I ever had for any woman. It was much easier to tell myself that you had tricked me, that you were not who I believed you to be. Anything to lessen my attachment for you. But nothing worked. I had already begun to love you, though I was too much of a fool to see it. When you said you were leaving I told myself it was best—that you, like everyone else in my life, would leave eventually, and it was better if you did it sooner than later. I knew the moment you'd gone, the moment you forfeited the company, that I was the only liar among the two of us. I had lied to myself. I know you don't feel the same way, but I can make you happy. We can be a family."

"Marco." She threw her arms around his neck and kissed his face—the face that she loved so painfully. "I love you too—so much!"

"But you left."

"I know. I was an even bigger idiot than you were," she said, laughing through her tears. "I was afraid that by staying, by loving you, I would become my mother—that I would lose myself in an effort to gain your affection. I was arrogant enough to think that I was not at all affected by my childhood, that you were the one who needed to learn about love. But I was just as guilty of bringing the past in, of returning to old hurts and using them to shield myself from hurt. I was a big coward."

"No bigger than I was. When you left I lost myself. I had never felt such pain—not even after losing my mother. I knew I had made a mistake—the biggest of my life—driving you away. I wanted to beg you to stay then, but I knew I wouldn't be able to face it if I threw myself on the ground before you and you left anyway. Like my mother did."

Her heart clenched. "Oh, Marco. I'm so sorry." She cradled his head against her breast. A momentary surge of rage at the woman who had hurt Marco so badly nearly stole her joy. "The past has a lot to make up for."

"I think we can start now. We're building a strong future." He put his hand on her stomach.

"Why did you give me the company, Marco?"

"Because it was what you wanted. And I wanted you to be happy, even if your happiness did not lie with me. At least that's what I told myself. But today…I couldn't stay away any longer." He leaned in from his position on the floor and kissed her gently on the lips—a kiss of barely leashed passion, a kiss of love. "I'd like it if we could work at rebuilding Chapman Electronics together. I love how your mind works. I'd love a chance to see you in action."

"What about when the baby comes?"

"We'll do whatever you think is best. We can put a daycare facility in the building, or we could alternate days so that one of us is always with him."

Her eyes widened. "Well, that's very progressive of you. I think you might be getting enlightened."

"Don't let it get around."

"I would never try to damage your formidable reputa-tion." She slid out of her chair and knelt with him on the floor, wrapping her arms tightly around him. "I don't know exactly what I want to do after I have the baby. I'm sure I'll want to stay home for a few months at least. But I am also sure that I love you, and that I want to spend the rest of my life with you. So what do you think?"

"I think—" he pressed a kiss to her neck "—that marriage is the only logical course of action."

She laughed. "Oh, is that right?"

"Mmm." He trailed kisses from just beneath her ear down to her collarbone, swirling his tongue in the hollow at the base of her neck. "I've done my research." He flicked the buttons of her blouse open.

She sucked in a breath as he feathered kisses over the swell of her breasts. "Have you?"

"Yes. And according to my research you and I are destined to be together forever and ever."

"Is that so?" she gasped.

"It's an indisputable fact. My figures are always accurate." He nipped her neck and she melted into him.

"And how did you arrive at your conclusion?"

"It's very simple. I love you. And I will love you, and honor you, and cherish you, for all of my days."

Coming Next Month

from **Harlequin Presents® EXTRA.** Available October 12, 2010.

#121 POWERFUL GREEK, HOUSEKEEPER WIFE
Robyn Donald
The Greek Tycoons

#122 THE GOOD GREEK WIFE?
Kate Walker
The Greek Tycoons

#123 BOARDROOM RIVALS, BEDROOM FIREWORKS!
Kimberly Lang
Back in His Bed

#124 UNFINISHED BUSINESS WITH THE DUKE
Heidi Rice
Back in His Bed

Coming Next Month

from **Harlequin Presents®.** Available October 26, 2010.

#2951 THE PREGNANCY SHOCK
Lynne Graham
The Drakos Baby

#2952 SOPHIE AND THE SCORCHING SICILIAN
Kim Lawrence
The Balfour Brides

#2953 FALCO: THE DARK GUARDIAN
Sandra Marton
The Orsini Brothers

#2954 CHOSEN BY THE SHEIKH
Kim Lawrence and Lynn Raye Harris

#2955 THE SABBIDES SECRET BABY
Jacqueline Baird

#2956 CASTELLANO'S MISTRESS OF REVENGE
Melanie Milburne

LARGER-PRINT BOOKS!

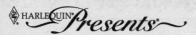

GET 2 FREE LARGER-PRINT
NOVELS PLUS 2 FREE GIFTS!

YES! Please send me 2 FREE LARGER-PRINT Harlequin Presents® novels and my 2 FREE gifts (gifts are worth about $10). After receiving them, if I don't wish to receive any more books, I can return the shipping statement marked "cancel". If I don't cancel, I will receive 6 brand-new novels every month and be billed just $4.55 per book in the U.S. or $5.24 per book in Canada. That's a saving of at least 13% off the cover price! It's quite a bargain! Shipping and handling is just 50¢ per book.* I understand that accepting the 2 free books and gifts places me under no obligation to buy anything. I can always return a shipment and cancel at any time. Even if I never buy another book, the two free books and gifts are mine to keep forever.

176/376 HDN E5NG

Name	(PLEASE PRINT)

Address	Apt. #

City	State/Prov.	Zip/Postal Code

Signature (if under 18, a parent or guardian must sign)

Mail to the **Harlequin Reader Service:**
IN U.S.A.: P.O. Box 1867, Buffalo, NY 14240-1867
IN CANADA: P.O. Box 609, Fort Erie, Ontario L2A 5X3

Not valid for current subscribers to Harlequin Presents Larger-Print books.

**Are you a subscriber to Harlequin Presents books
and want to receive the larger-print edition?
Call 1-800-873-8635 today!**

* Terms and prices subject to change without notice. Prices do not include applicable taxes. Sales tax applicable in N.Y. Canadian residents will be charged applicable provincial taxes and GST. Offer not valid in Quebec. This offer is limited to one order per household. All orders subject to approval. Credit or debit balances in a customer's account(s) may be offset by any other outstanding balance owed by or to the customer. Please allow 4 to 6 weeks for delivery. Offer available while quantities last.

Your Privacy: Harlequin Books is committed to protecting your privacy. Our Privacy Policy is available online at www.eHarlequin.com or upon request from the Reader Service. From time to time we make our lists of customers available to reputable third parties who may have a product or service of interest to you. If you would prefer we not share your name and address, please check here. ☐

Help us get it right—We strive for accurate, respectful and relevant communications. To clarify or modify your communication preferences, visit us at www.ReaderService.com/consumerschoice.

HPLP10R

HARLEQUIN®

A Romance

FOR EVERY MOOD™

Spotlight on

Inspirational

Wholesome romances
that touch the heart and soul.

See the next page
to enjoy a sneak peek from
the Love Inspired® Suspense
inspirational series.

*See below for a sneak peek from
our inspirational line, Love Inspired® Suspense*

*Enjoy this heart-stopping excerpt from
RUNNING BLIND
by top author Shirlee McCoy,
available November 2010!*

**The mission trip to Mexico was supposed to be an
adventure. But the thrill turns sour when Jenna Dougherty
and her roommate Magdalena are kidnapped.**

"It's okay. I'm here to help." The voice was as deep as the
darkness, but Jenna Dougherty didn't believe the lie. She
could do nothing but lie still as hands slid down her arms,
felt the rope around her wrists.

"I'm going to use a knife to cut you free, Jenna. Hold
still."

The cold blade of a knife pressed close to her head before
her gag fell away.

"I—" she started, but her mouth was dry, and she could
do nothing but suck in air.

"Shhh. Whatever needs to be said can be said when
we're out of here." Nick spoke quietly, his hand gentle on
her cheek. There and gone as he sliced through the ropes on
her wrists and ankles.

He pulled her upright. "Come on. We may be on
borrowed time."

"I can't leave my friend," Jenna rasped out.

"There's no one here. Just us."

"She has to be here." Jenna took a step away.

"There's no one here. Let's go before that changes."

"It's dark. Maybe if we find a light…"

"What did you say?"

"We need to turn on the light. I can't leave until I know that—"

"What can you see, Jenna?"

"Nothing."

"No shadows? No light?"

"No."

"It's broad daylight. There's light spilling in from the window I climbed in through. You can't see it?"

She went cold at his words.

"I can't see anything."

"You've got a nasty bruise on your forehead. Maybe that has something to do with it." His fingers traced the tender flesh on her forehead.

"It doesn't matter *how* it happened. I'm blind!"

Can Nick help Jenna find her friend or will chasing this trail have Jenna running blindly again into danger?

Find out in RUNNING BLIND, available in November 2010 only from Love Inspired Suspense.

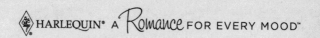